Stasiland

STASI LAND

Rolf Richardson

Matador
9 Priory Business Park,
Wistow Road, Kibworth Beauchamp,
Leicestershire. LE8 0RX
Tel: 0116 279 2299
Email: books@troubador.co.uk
Web: www.troubador.co.uk/matador
Twitter: @matadorbooks

ISBN 978 1789018 028

British Library Cataloguing in Publication Data.
A catalogue record for this book is available from the British Library.

Typeset in 10.5pt Adobe Garamond Pro by Troubador Publishing Ltd, Leicester, UK

Matador is an imprint of Troubador Publishing Ltd

One

If Johann Kästner had to die, he could not have chosen a better place. The burghers of Saxony were proud of their Upper Elbe scenery, far superior in their view to the more famous River Rhine. The Lorelei? Rubbish! Not a patch on the Bastei. That Kästner had also arranged for his demise to take place in one of their superb old paddle steamers was icing on the cake.

Which vessel to choose? The fleet's Methuselah, the Stadt Wehlen, built in 1879? Or the Meissen from 1885? Maybe the Kurort Rathen dating from 1896? Even the baby of the fleet, the 1929 Leipzig? There were nine possibilities.

Of course I'm being frivolous in suggesting Kästner had any say in selecting where he wanted to shuffle off this mortal coil. It was pure chance, dictated by the Saxon Steamship Company's timetable. Any premature death is a tragedy – and Johann was only 35 – but life is a joke anyway, so one might as well treat his end with levity.

It was also pure chance that found me aboard the same vessel at the same time; an unlikely conjunction, but again, life is little more than a series of coincidences.

For my presence there I blame Maggie, my ex-wife. We had spent the past twenty-five years blaming each other for just about everything, so why stop now? When our two children left the nest, the tenuous bonds that had kept us together finally snapped. Maggie stayed in the house, allowing me to keep the silver Porsche; an inequitable division of spoils, you might think, but by this time I was prepared to agree to almost anything to get her off my back.

I could afford to be generous. If I had been unlucky in love, the gods had made up for it by allowing me some success in business. I won't bore you with the details; but suffice it to say, I had enough stashed away to keep me in comfort until the day I received my centenary telegram from the Queen – or, more likely, an email from the King.

Freed of the burdens of family and the need to earn a crust, I did a Peter Pan; regressed to youth. Every kid in the country now has their inalienable right to a Gap year, extended by some to a Gap lifetime. At the ripe old age of fifty-five, Ed Blake – that's me – would join the Gap club; for however long I pleased and with the help of my trusty Porsche.

The years had wrought some changes. I could now think of nothing worse than the teenage utopia of slumming it on a tropical beach, while listening to rap music and indulging in unlimited sex. My Gap would be more civilised, more cultural. The timing was perfect. It was early June and I would set out to explore the cradle of civilisation: the continent of Europe.

I became a weather fanatic, every day studying the forecasts. What was the intention of that damned jet-stream? If it looked like funnelling depressions across northern Europe, I would dodge south of the Alps, where summers are more stable. But if a dry spell was in prospect over France, Benelux, Germany, the Czech Republic, Slovakia and Hungary, that's where I would start.

So far I had been lucky; nothing worse than a thunderstorm over Bruges and some iffy weather in Koblenz. I liked to settle in one place for a few days and cover the local area before moving on. It was with this in mind that I had checked in to the Hotel Lindtner. The location? As I was destined to stay much longer than intended, under circumstances that were, to say the least, unusual, I'll protect its anonymity and only say it lay on the River Elbe, somewhere between Dresden and the Czech border. Let's just call it 'Die Stadt'; The Town.

Two

Day one at the Lindtner had been devoted to the area's main attraction, the Bastei: a rockface rising 600ft from the river. As this aspect was almost vertical and thus off limits to all but mountaineers equipped with crampons, ordinary tourists were directed round the back to a car park near the summit. From there we could take a series of walks through a jumble of weird sandstone monoliths, eventually to emerge high above the Elbe, with spectacular views.

I had dutifully done this and returned to Die Stadt for a beer and snack lunch before exploring the town itself, which spread up the hill from a narrow shelf of land by the river. The temperature was in the mid-twenties; the sun was shining. With high season almost upon us, the main square was humming with humans intent on enjoying themselves. Maggie and my marital problems were a million miles away. This was the life!

I perked up even more when enquiring at reception about a good place to have dinner. On duty was Frau Lindtner, whom I had not met until then and who asked to be called Trudi. From the surname I took her to be the owner, the hotel a family affair. She was a comfortably upholstered lady of average height, probably mid-fifties, with longish blonde hair. Had I been God, I might have designed her oval face with a less prominent nose and slimmed down that bone structure, but maybe it was just these imperfections that made her attractive. Or maybe, in my newly liberated state, I was promoting *any* female with an age still in double figures into a nymphette.

Get a grip on yourself, Ed, I told myself. The lady in front of me was just an ordinary hotel owner, wearing a smart blue dress and the smile she lavished on every customer.

My German is adequate rather than brilliant, so when travelling in the old Western part, where English is often spoken better than in Britain, I tend to gravitate to *my* mother tongue. However, Trudi came from what had comically been called the German Democratic Republic. Any country that includes the word 'democratic' in its title is, by definition, the worst kind of dictatorship, and here the real rulers had been the secret police, the Staatsicherheitsdienst, known to one and all as the Stasi. Die Stadt had languished for 44 years in Communist Stasiland, where the second language had been Russian; English that of the enemy. Youngsters were catching up fast, but older folk still found it hard, so Trudi abandoned her halting English and we fell back on *her* mother tongue.

My hostess had recommended not only an excellent riverside restaurant for dinner, but also insisted I absolutely *must* take a trip on one of their famous paddle steamers. Upstream is best, she said. Past the Bastei, which you will now see from another angle; after that, riverside villages like Kurort Rathen. Get off at Königstein. Take the bus up to the castle, without doubt the most impressive in Germany. Was she a wee bit biased? And return by train. A wonderful day out.

Not only was Trudi's enthusiasm infectious, it was exactly the sort of day I would have chosen myself: nice scenery, a dash of culture and history, and a forecast of wall-to-wall sunshine. Eat your heart out, Maggie! This was bliss.

Fortified by a solid night's sleep and with expectations high, I arrived next morning on Die Stadt's quayside. A frequent source of dispute is the amount of water that comes across the border, only a few miles upstream. The Czechs point out they have no control over the amount of precipitation the Almighty decides to pour over central Europe, while the Germans reply that flood damage could be reduced if the Czechs made some attempt at river management. Now, in June, with snow melt long gone and a preceding spell of dry weather, the river was at an acceptable level; high enough for steamers to ply their trade, low enough to be well away from habitation.

It was on this gently sloping floodplain, between the town and landing stage, that we waited for our transport up-river. There were perhaps a couple of dozen people milling around, amongst them a father and young son, kicking a ball about. What primeval trigger makes booting a spherical object so irresistible? There's no obvious survival benefit. But if a group of people even *see* a ball, they *have to* start belting it.

It was all very casual. Just killing time. I happened to be nearby when a small, round, black and white object – hardly FIFA approved, but rolling nicely – began heading for the water. So I came to the rescue; kicked it back up the slope to Dad and his lad. Which prompted Dad to indicate they could do with another team member. "Die Stadt United". Just until our steamer arrived.

The father was a slim man in his thirties with a mop of unruly dark hair. The front of his black T-shirt had an image of a Teutonic knight, kitted out in full armour and spear; on the back, the words "Wacht am Rhein"; it looked like a tailor-made piece of clothing. His young number two wore a blue top with "HERTHA" in block capitals on the front; and "Die Alte Dame" on the back. No ambiguity here; the kid supported Hertha, a Berlin football club, known as Die Alte Dame – The Old Lady. If our steamer didn't turn up soon, he'd be old enough to play for them.

Sometimes the most innocent of actions can have far-reaching consequences. Had I known what was in store when I rescued this ball from its unintended drift towards Dresden, I might have thought twice about it. But, with no oracle to foretell the future, I simply did my good deed for the day.

Twenty minutes later our transport came into view; a slender white vessel with light green lines running fore and aft. She had a black funnel with a white collar two-thirds of the way up. Propulsion was by a pair of paddles amidships. The words on the bows and around the paddle housing told us it was the 'Kurort Rathen'.

As we lined up to present our tickets, dad turned to me and held out his hand; Germans tend to be more formal than Brits: "Name's Jonny. Thanks for joining us. Karl's going to be Hertha's striker, so needs all the practice he can get. Not that he stands much of a chance the way the damned Bundesliga's going; all Turks and blacks from Africa. Don't seem to want good German lads."

Not an argument to get involved in, so I let it go. Forgot about it as we scurried on board to find the best seats, which was not that easy because the boat had started her journey three hours and several stops earlier in Dresden.

In this weather the saloons were almost empty, most people keen to enjoy the scenery from one of the open decks. I managed to find a seat up front, where there was no canopy, and sat down to enjoy the ride.

As Trudi had forecast, we soon passed the Bastei. I craned my neck to see where I had been the previous day. We then stopped at Kurort Rathen, our ship's home port; 'Kurort' means 'Cure Place' – a health resort or spa. In the sunshine it looked an attractive spot, with turreted lookouts on a rocky outcrop and a row of sunshades hosting a clutch of beer drinkers. We moored next to the 'Bergland': a ferry?

After a quick exchange of passengers we left Kurort Rathen for Königstein, where I would be getting off to visit what Trudi had described as 'the best castle in Germany'. After that, a train back to base.

I started to feel fidgety; fancied a change from gawking at scenery. During my initial hunt for a seat, I recalled passing the engine room, where the full works lay open for inspection.

According to the blurb, it was an 'oil-fed oscillating steam engine', spotlessly maintained, with lots of copper piping and ancient instruments, the housing painted green and red.

I left my seat and ambled back for another look at the engine room, but this time stared down in disbelief.

Another sort of red, rather darker, was seeping from under a figure that lay face down on top of the Kurort Rathen's immaculate works. His feet were spread out, arms hanging down, as if embracing the cogs and pistons. In large letters on his T-shirt were the words "Wacht am Rhein".

It was my football friend, Jonny. Bile rose in my gullet. The paddles were throbbing away, driven by… what was it again? An oscillating steam engine. Jonny was oscillating on top, in a macabre parody of the sexual act. With no apparent effect on the engine's efficiency.

I was absurdly slow on the uptake. Just stood there, mesmerised. Those words stared back at me: "Wacht am Rhein": Watch on the Rhine. What the hell was that supposed to mean?

Why was I fixating on some weird words when I was confronted by a much stranger puzzle? What, in God's name, was Jonny doing, apparently very dead, in the Kurort Rathen's engine room?

Movement beside me signalled I was no longer alone.

"Jesus!" It was one of the crew, a beer paunch wrapped in a grey shirt, jowly face on top. I put him in his forties, thinning black hair and dark eyes; a night club bouncer going to seed.

He looked at me, appalled. Gasped: "What the fuck have you done?"

"What have *I* done…?

It took some seconds for the extent of my predicament to sink in.

Three

"He has a son," I said, pointing at Jonny, who was quietly bleeding to death – actually, he looked to be already gone.

Beer-Gut gave me a glance that said: 'guy's totally bonkers'. Who could blame him. It looked as though I was responsible and was now wittering away about some son. As I could scarcely abscond in mid river, Beer-Gut just shrugged and departed, no doubt to tell his captain the good news.

Why was my attention now focussed on Hertha football club's young hopeful? It was absurd. But my brain was darting off in strange directions. It seemed important that I locate Kurt… no, the name was Karl, before his dad's death became common knowledge.

I made my way swiftly to the aft deck. If I drew a blank there, he would have to be on the upper midships. I found him in the rearmost row of seats talking to a large matronly lady.

"Here's the Arsenal fan," he announced as I approached.

During our kickabout Karl had asked which club I supported. With no particular sporting allegiance, but having lived in the south of England, on a whim I'd picked Arsenal. In Karl's eyes I was now a certified Arsenal fan.

Having found Jonny's son, I had no idea what to say. Could hardly blurt out that his father was lying face down in the engine room.

In desperation, I knocked the ball back to his court and asked: "Seen your dad recently?"

Karl shook his head, uninterested.

"I think he was last seen chatting to another man," volunteered the large lady who seemed to have befriended the boy.

'Another man'; that might be interesting, so I tried Karl again. "Can you remember what your dad's friend looked like?"

Again he shook his head, this time more sulkily. From my time as father of a young boy – Karl must have been around ten – I remembered they could be tricky to handle.

Further efforts to prize anything out of the lad were put on hold by our tour guide coming back on the public address. A bubbly young lady, she had been keeping us up to date on the passing highlights and here she was again; first in German, then in English:

"Ladies and gentlemen, we shall soon be arriving in Königstein, where many of you will be getting off to visit one of our famous castles. However, I have to advise you of a short delay, while the authorities come on board. Nothing to worry about and we'll soon be on our way again. But until this inspection is complete, we ask you to stay in your seats. No standing in the gangways, please. For those leaving us at Königstein, we will tell you when you may disembark."

A curious buzz filled the air.

"Wonder what this is all about," mused Karl's mother-figure.

I kept my counsel. Not for me to say that anyone roaming around the gangways would be treated to a spectacle not in the tour script: a corpse in the engine room. I wondered how the crew would cover up this piece of unpleasantness.

The next 20 minutes, before our arrival at Königstein, were surreal. Alone amongst the passengers, I knew what it was all about. The captain would have phoned ahead and requested a police presence for our arrival; Beer-Gut would no doubt then point me out as the chief suspect. Quite possibly their *only* suspect. There was little I could do except wait.

To further complicate matters, Karl became fractious. He may have started out being off-hand about his missing father, but this bravery was now beginning to wear thin.

"Want to find dad," he announced. And started running up the deck.

Beer-Gut, who was standing amidships ensuring we obeyed orders, stopped him.

"Go back to Mum, little one," he said, not unkindly.

"She's *not* my Mum." Karl stomped back, his temper rising.

I wondered where his mother was. The most likely answer was a broken marriage, Dad taking advantage of some legally allotted quality time with his son.

"Your mother not here?" enquired the lady, his stand-in parent.

"'Course not," replied Karl, rudely. "You can see she isn't."

"Well, let me be your mother for a while."

She tried to gather the lad to her bosom, only to have him break free and make for me.

"He's an Arsenal fan," he said, as if this explained everything.

Stand-in mother took the rebuff with philosophical raised eyebrows: "That makes all the difference, of course."

The young boy stood in front of me. Shyly. I might have been a fellow football fan, but was still a stranger.

"Can *you* help me find Papa?" he asked.

"Later," I replied. "You heard what the lady said: we must stay where we are until they let us leave."

"*Then* can we find Papa?"

"Of course." And felt an absolute heel. But what else could I say? Or do? In a few minutes everything would be revealed – at least to poor little Karl. I could only pretend that, like all the others, I knew nothing.

The boy relapsed into a moody silence. Sat on my knee. The Kurort Rathen paddled its way towards Königstein.

All the while Beer-Gut kept a close eye on us.

Four

Königstein, the castle, loomed menacingly above the River Elbe, as though trying to shut off our sunlight. Königstein, the town, also on our starboard side, lay at river level a little further on. Our mooring was obvious from some way off because of the presence of a distinctive blue and yellow vehicle. No flashing light, because it was stationary. But we were expected. By the police.

Our tour guide's estimate of being away again 'soon' proved optimistic. The law moved in a mysterious and leisurely way. I say 'mysterious' because we were rooted to our seats and could see little beyond a gaggle of conferring uniforms. After 20 minutes or so, a cover was placed over the engine room. More waiting for something to happen. A blue flashing light came speeding up and drew to a halt beside the first car. Reinforcements. Our passengers started to become impatient. Then annoyed. Then angry.

It must have been a good 40 minutes after our arrival that the public address finally came to life again. First with apologies for the delay. Then with the bad news. The 'Kurort Rathen's' cruise was at an end. Terminated. Would not be continuing to Bad Schandau, its intended destination. There followed some instructions for those who had booked all the way, but I was not listening. We were being allowed to leave. Indeed, forced to leave.

Like the others, I got up and prepared to abandon ship. Felt a tug on my arm.

"Where's Papa?" Karl was now close to tears.

"Seems you've been volunteered," said the lady who had befriended the lad. "Good luck."

So I took his hand: "Come on, Karl. Let's see what we can do."

I knew nothing about Jonny or his son beyond their first names. Not their surnames; not where they lived. Nothing. All I could do was hand Karl over to the police with an explanation. There should be a trained officer – usually a female – to deal with such delicate matters.

The departing queue of passengers moved slowly. There had been no explanation for the delay and subsequent cancellation, so there were plenty of disgruntled comments. I could understand the crew's reluctance to come up with the real reason, but someone should have dreamt up a plausible lie. Phoney but harmless information is better than no information at all.

Having been at the stern of the boat, Karl and I were the last to disembark. Two police were manning the gangway, while two others were on board scrutinising the departing passengers. One of these was a policewoman, and I was about to place Karl in her care when I heard a shout:

"That's him!" It was Beer-Gut. Pointing at me.

The two closest officers gripped my arms. This dislodged Karl's little hand from mine, at which he wailed: "Where's Papa?" And burst into tears.

"Now look what you've done!" I was incensed.

Nothing upsets proceedings better than a howling child. For a moment no one knew what to do. So I took the opportunity to add:

"This is Jonny's son, you idiots!"

"Jonny?"

"The guy in the engine room."

Slowly it dawned on them.

For a moment the grip on my arms loosened, so I bent down to the kid's level and said: "This nice lady will look after you, Karl. Promise you'll be brave boy?"

He nodded, still tearful, starting to realise something was seriously amiss.

"If you're really good, I'll take you to see Arsenal play. How about that?"

With a wan smile, he replied: "And you'll come to see Hertha?"

"It's a deal."

The policewoman took Karl's hand.

I straightened up and announced: "Now the boy's safe with you, I'm off to the castle."

I knew this was not going to happen, but why make it easy for them? I had nothing to do with Jonny's death and intended to make that plain from the outset.

The burly male officers renewed their grip on my arms. I tried to shake myself free. In vain.

I yelled: "What's all this about?"

"We just want to ask you a few questions, sir."

"Am I under arrest?"

"It'll be easier if you come with us, sir."

Having made my stand, I reckoned that was enough. No point in antagonising them any further. I allowed myself to be marched off the boat and into one of the waiting cars.

Behind me, I heard one of the officers growl: "Got a right bastard here. A killer *and* a paedophile."

My friendship with Karl had landed me in a second fine mess. I was not only a murderer but also a predator of little boys.

Not the sort of day I'd planned when setting off from the Hotel Lindtner a few hours earlier.

Five

The police were tight-lipped. Would only say we were going to Dresden. No talk of any arrest. Not yet.

The journey took longer than anticipated – nearly an hour and a half. This in spite of the fact that the German road system is about the best in the world. Although the first motorway had been built in Italy during the 1920s, it was Adolf who really set the ball rolling. A pity he didn't stick to such peaceful pursuits. By the outbreak of war in 1939 the autobahns were decades ahead of any other country. The mighty USA suffered from appalling roads right up until the late 1950s, when President Eisenhower, worried by the defence implications, signed the Interstate Highways Act. Britain has forever been playing catch-up, her roads never fully fit for purpose.

I loved driving the autobahns, with their unrestricted speeds on open sections, but it paid to keep your wits about you. About a hundred miles per hour was fast enough for me and my silver Porsche, but I was often left standing by apparently rocket-propelled Mercs.

Now even the autobahns were having difficulty coping with the relentless traffic increase. The Berliner-Ring, host to a million trucks shuttling between east and west, could be a nightmare. And sitting in the back of a Saxony police car, I discovered that the Dresdner-Ring – actually only a semi-circle – was as bad. The A4 northern section was in the grip of road works, the lorry lane near stationary, but eventually we peeled off and came to a stop outside a low, olive-coloured building; I guessed somewhere in the city's northern suburbs.

By now most of the day had passed since Trudi Lindtner's excellent breakfast; I'd had nothing more to eat and was feeling peckish. As much to impress on them my innocence as to actually get fed, I demanded dinner. Their reply was a brusque, single word: "Später". Later.

It soon became clear that the Saxony cops were as keen to get stuck into their evening meal as I was. All they needed was a routine confession from their latest criminal – me – and it would be home to Mum and everyone could relax. With this in mind, they dumped me in a windowless interview room, guarded by a single uniformed officer, who was joined almost immediately by two men in plain clothes.

The younger of the two took a deferential seat to the right, a little behind the fellow who was clearly the boss – a large and unfit-looking elderly man, who must have been close to retirement; his fingers were nicotine stained and he had the testy air of a man constantly craving another fix.

He introduced himself as Inspector Kirst, adding a casual wave towards his number two, whose name I did not catch. These brief formalities out of the way, he pushed a photo across the table and asked: "Do you know this man?"

It was Jonny, looking a great deal better than when I'd last seen him.

I nodded.

"Out loud, please, so your reply can be recorded."

Although my passport was back in the hotel, my identity had been established by a British driving licence. Even so, all exchanges so far had been in German, probably because I spoke it reasonably well. The inspector looked old enough to have started his career while Dresden was still in the Communist east, in which case his Russian was probably better than his English.

I was happy enough to continue in German but had to be careful. Any linguistic confusion could cost me. So I replied:

"I met Jonny for the first and only time this morning. Played some football with him and his son. So certainly didn't *know* him."

The Inspector made no comment. Retrieved the photo and produced a piece of paper. Waved it at me and said:

I have here a signed statement from Josef Feldmann, who says he found you standing over the body of Johann Kästner…"

"Johann Kästner?"

"The deceased. Who preferred to be known as Jonny. When crew member Feldmann challenged you, he says you confessed to killing him."

"I did no such thing!"

For a moment, Inspector Kirst looked nonplussed. In his hand was a signed affidavit claiming to have heard a confession to the killing. Now it no longer looked so simple. Our respective evening meals began to disappear into the distance.

Kirst gathered himself, consulted the statement again and said:

"According to crew member Feldmann, when he found you standing over the body, he said: 'My God, what have you done…'"

"…Actually, he said: 'What the fuck have you done?'"

"Whatever…" The Inspector did not like interruptions, glared at me and continued: "Feldmann claims you then replied, 'I did it'."

"Your witness seems to make a habit of getting things wrong," I replied. "I can't remember my exact words, but they were on the lines of 'What have *I* done? Stress on the word 'I'. Absolute astonishment. I was *denying* being the culprit."

Kirst frowned, uncertain how to proceed, so I decided to throw him a lifeline:

"You will appreciate, Inspector, that my German is not as good as it ought to be. Easy for Feldmann to misunderstand."

Kirst tapped the table with a pen, pondered for a few moments, then said: "Are you saying, Herr Blake, that you did *not* kill Johann Kästner?"

"Correct. I spent a few minutes kicking a ball about with him and his son. That's all. Hardly a motive for murder."

More pondering from the Inspector. It dawned on me that he had a problem, because his Königstein colleagues had assumed they already had the murderer: me. Beer-Gut Feldmann told them I had confessed, so they looked no further. I had seen no evidence of officers taking any names, so could only assume that everyone else on board, including the killer, had been allowed to disappear into the wide blue yonder. Understandable, but sloppy police work.

It didn't need much of a denial from me to convince the Inspector they had got it horribly wrong. The chances of a respectable, middle-aged Englishman suddenly deciding to kill a man he had never met before were vanishingly small. As no one had been seen jumping from the boat and swimming frantically to the shore, it had to be assumed the person responsible had disembarked at Königstein. And been allowed to disappear.

Perhaps in an effort to salvage something from this disaster, Kirst continued:

"There's also the question of your inappropriate behaviour towards Karl, the deceased's son."

"What do you mean 'inappropriate'?"

Kirst squirmed. "Elderly men befriending young boys… their motives must be suspect."

Being described as 'elderly' – me, a youthful fifty-five – was annoying, but unimportant. I had to hit this paedophilia nonsense on the head. In slow and measured tones, I informed him:

"While waiting for our boat to arrive, I was invited by Jonny – Herr Kästner – to join him and his son in some casual football. Later, when I made the horrific discovery of his body in the engine room, I immediately thought of little Karl. There had been no obvious Mrs. Kästner, so this kid would presumably now be alone on the boat, not knowing his father had just been killed. As the only person he knew – albeit only slightly, I felt I had a duty of care. Wouldn't you agree?"

It would be difficult to *disagree*, but the Inspector merely sat there, tapping the table with his pen. More pondering.

I asked: "By the way, what happened to young Karl? I left him with one of your policewomen."

"He's back with his mother."

"Ah. So he has a mother."

"Of course. Mrs. Kästner. Separated from her husband, but still legally married, I believe."

"That's a relief." With no further reaction from the constabulary, I continued: "I've had a stressful day, so I'd like to return to my hotel. If you don't mind."

Kirst appeared to mind a lot, but having no reason to detain me just scowled. Then, after an abrupt "Moment" – like "hang on a minute" in English – he made a follow-me gesture to his number two and they left the room. A fleeting grin from the uniformed officer, who had been sitting in on our talk, led me to suppose the Inspector was not universally popular.

The two of us sat there in the interview room for a good five minutes, metaphorically twiddling our thumbs. When the two detectives returned, the Inspector announced: "You're free to go."

I got up: "That's kind of you." My sarcasm made no impression, so I added: "However, my car is back at the hotel. I'm stuck in… wherever this is, with no obvious way of getting back."

I suspect Kirst was about to say something like 'Tough luck buddy, you're on your own', but his number two, who until then had remained dumb, piped up:

"One of our Bad Schandau cars is still here. Due to return at any moment. Could easily drop off Herr Blake."

Bad Schandau, the nearest town of any size to Königstein, would have been where the police that met the Kurort Rathen were based. They were now due to go home.

Kirst had one parting shot: "We may need to ask some more questions, so don't leave the area."

"How long might that be?" I'd been planning to move on again quite soon.

"No idea. We'll let you know."

I had no chance of arguing the point, because Inspector Kirst was gone. With no more words. And no apology.

I got out my mobile and phoned the Hotel Lindtner.

It was answered by Trudi. I told her I hoped to be back within a couple of hours, depending on the traffic, and was starving. Could she please make sure they didn't close the dining room if I was a bit late?

"How was the castle?" she asked.

"Never got there. I've spent the afternoon in a murder inquiry."

"You've *what?*"

"I'll explain when I see you." And rang off.

Six

I arrived back at my hotel just before the restaurant closed and was greeted by Frau Lindtner herself, who showed me to a table. She was flushed and excited – which made her even more attractive – and whispered:

"Since you phoned we've been hearing all sorts of rumours about the Kurort Rathen being met by the police at Königstein. Were you involved?"

"I'm afraid so."

"I'm busy right now, but would love to hear about it. Let's have a chat when things calm down. Say, in an hour or so. When you've finished your meal."

Nothing like a juicy scandal to liven up an average day, so I indicated this would be acceptable.

She dashed off with a coy smile and wagging finger: "Now, don't run away."

I realised how serious this admonition was when the waiter

came to take my order. Madam had told him I could have a bottle of wine on the house. With such a seduction there was no risk of me running away. I was not one to gulp my drink, and after a full bottle I'd be anyone's.

I settled down in companionable solitude to do justice to the hotel's excellent dinner and to review what had been an extraordinary day with a mass of unanswered questions.

Some of these answers should surface pretty quickly.

Jonny and Karl had boarded the boat with me, so were probably locals; Trudi should know something about them. And the manner of Jonny's death was not likely to remain a mystery for long. I had only been able to see a sprawling body apparently leaking some dark liquid, which was unlikely to have been engine oil. However, the media would soon be in full cry and I'd be willing to bet that by tomorrow evening the autopsy findings would be known to every man woman and child in Germany.

What about the 'Wacht am Rhein' on Jonny's T-shirt? People often dressed in silly slogans that had nothing to do with them, but these words were so unusual I felt they must mean something. Maybe Trudi could throw some light on it.

The biggest 'why' of all was the most difficult to answer. *Why* had Jonny Kästner been killed? And by whom? Inspector Kirst was clearly floundering. But it was early days.

I was the only guest left in the dining room when Trudi reappeared. The evening rush now over, she was ready to hear about the day's big event.

"Off you go. I'll clear up here," she told the waiter, who was removing the last of my debris; well, not quite the last, because I'd lost the alcoholic stamina of youth and my bottle of wine was still half full.

The waiter disappeared into the kitchen, while Trudi locked the dining room door from the inside, grabbed a wine glass from a cabinet and filled it from the remains of my bottle, said: "There's more where this came from if we're still thirsty," then sat down opposite me.

Trudi Lindtner must have been around my age, handsome rather than pretty, solid rather than fat. She had straight blonde hair down to her shoulders, blue-grey eyes and a mouth that looked to have had plenty of experience in the things that mouths do: laughing, eating and…? I wondered if there was – had ever been – a Herr Lindtner.

She started on her wine and said: "Tell me all about it."

I gave her the full saga, from the moment I met Jonny and his boy until my arrival back at the hotel in the police car.

"This'll bring the press and TV along. Should fill the place up nicely." Ever the businesswoman.

"So the Kästners were locals?" I asked.

"I believe Jonny moved to Dresden a while back. After some sort of argument. As far as I know, Josie and the boy still live in the family house a short way out of town."

"What was Jonny's job? Anything that might lead him to such a ghastly fate?"

"Don't know whether you'd call it a job, but Jonny Kästner was well known as the leader of a political party: the German Democratic Right, the DDR."

"Might that have got him killed?"

"They're pretty extreme."

"In what way?"

"Germany for Germans. Kick out the migrants. That sort of thing.

"Sound a nasty lot."

"Maybe. But Jonny wasn't at all nasty."

"Seemed okay to me too," I said. "Just an ordinary dad out for the day with his son."

Trudi nodded. "Jonny made DDR policies sound… well, almost sensible. He was very popular."

"So why murder him?"

She shrugged. "Who knows?"

I mulled this over for a moment, then asked: "His T-shirt had a fierce-looking medieval knight on the front. And the words 'Wacht am Rhein' on the back. What might that mean?"

"Wacht am Rhein… It's a poem. A song. Written when they were trying to invent what became Germany. Popular whenever there was a war. Especially… well…"

"The last one?" I prompted.

She nodded, embarrassed: "Nowadays, it's hardly ever heard."

"Except when seen on Jonny's T-shirt."

She nodded again. "He was mister nice guy in charge of a party that's in business to stir things."

"What's this 'Wacht am Rhein' about? Can you remember the words?"

"Not the verses – there were lots of them. But the chorus comes back so often it's difficult to forget."

She said no more. Needed a verbal shove. So I said:

"Don't be shy. I'd like to hear it."

"The song?"

"Please."

Trudi lubricated her larynx with another shot of red and began:

"Lieb Vaterland, magst ruhig sein,

lieb Vaterland, magst ruhig sein;

Fest steht und treu die Wacht,

die Wacht am Rhein!

Fest steht und treu die Wacht,

die Wacht am Rhein!"

It was one of those spooky moments. Shivers ran down my spine. Just the two of us in an otherwise empty room, as Trudi Lindtner's lovely voice re-created the drug that had driven the Kaiser's men out of the trenches during the first war. And fuelled Hitler's divisions in the second.

In English, the words look harmless enough:

"Dear Fatherland, be calm (sung twice),

Firm stands and true the Watch, the Watch on the Rhine (sung twice)."

But in German, and set to a stirring tune, they were magic.

Every country has its martial music: France, *La Marseillaise*; Britain, *Jerusalem* and *Rule Britannia*; Germany is up there amongst the best with the Nazi *Horst Wessel* song and *Wacht am Rhein*. Melodious drugs that could drive normally sensible men to feats of madness.

"Why the Rhine?" I asked. "Why the watch on that particular river?"

Trudi smiled: "It was written in the mid-1800s, when Napoleon had only recently been put away and the German-speaking people were still a collection of small states. Not yet a nation. The bogeyman was France, the enemy across the Rhine. Since then the song has come to warn of enemies wherever they may appear."

"Jonny Kästner, knight in armour, dedicated to protecting Germany from its enemies," I mused.

She nodded slowly: So why suspect *you* as his assassin?"

"Only because Feldmann found me at the scene of the crime and jumped to the wrong conclusion. Even Inspector Kirst, not my greatest fan, soon realised I could have had nothing to do with it."

"Then why still insist you must not leave here?"

"It's called shutting the stable door after the horse has bolted. Kirst's men at Königstein, thinking they had the case nicely wrapped up, made the mistake of letting everyone off the boat, without noting their names and addresses. Kirst has to be seen to be doing *something* right, so he can't let his only witness go. Not at once. But he'll have to let me off the hook in a day or two."

"You hope. Meanwhile, what will you do?"

I shrugged. "Go for walks. Inspect the local area."

"Which you've already done. So the Hotel Lindtner has an offer to stop you getting bored. High season is upon us; we could do with another helping hand; and reliable staff are hard to find." She smiled, invitingly.

"The person you're thinking of would be hopelessly *un*-reliable: he'd be off again as soon as the cops gave their consent."

"Maybe. But every little helps. Think about it."

I found Trudi's offer intriguing. Her flirty manner even more so. I got up, thanked her for the free wine and said:

"I will. Think about it. In my little attic den. Perhaps you'd like to help by tucking me up in bed."

For a moment I thought I might have misjudged the mood. Gone too far. But there was no slap across the chops. Instead, she appeared to give my suggestion serious thought; finally, smiled and said:

"You've had enough excitement for one day. Let's talk again in the morning."

Seven

Next morning Trudi was not around – presumably on hotel business – and I had an attack of itchy feet. The forecast was for the weather to break in a couple of days, so I wanted to make the most of the sunshine. I took Inspector Kirst's request to mean merely that I must *reside* in the local area; what I did during the day was up to me.

My obvious target was the place I had failed to reach yesterday: Königstein. River transport had proved a mite too deadly, so I decided to give my silver Porsche a run. After a short double-back towards Dresden for the nearest bridge over the Elbe, I parked in Königstein town shortly before eleven. Then took the shuttle bus up the hill to the castle.

The area enclosed by the battlements was wide and open with just a few buildings, none of which lived up to Trudi's hype. However, the views from the battlements were spectacular; the Elbe describing a graceful curve far below. I watched as a paddle steamer edged towards the landing stage, then moored up; maybe the Kurort Rathen again, too far away to tell. I had a tasty snack lunch, walked down into town for the exercise and was back at the Lindtner just after four.

I found a message in my pigeon-hole: "*Chief Inspector Fischer would like to talk to you. Please meet him in the hotel bar at 6.30.*"

I was now worth a *Chief* Inspector; a rise in the ranks. Would this new fellow be an improvement on Inspector Kirst?

I turned up at the appointed time. On such a fine evening most people were outside, only one person in the bar, a young fellow in shorts; obviously not the Chief Inspector. I was about to go out again when he waved me over, got up as I approached and held out his hand.

"Good of you to come, Mr. Blake. I'm Chief Inspector Helmut Fischer."

A bigger contrast could not be imagined. This man was lean and fit, a good twenty years younger than Kirst, whom he outranked. Again unlike Kirst, he addressed me in impeccable English.

I must have looked confused, because he apologised, removed an ID from his pocket and said: "My credentials".

The document was headed 'Bundeskriminalamt'; its logo a bird-like creature that looked to be punching the air with both fists. The name was 'Polizei Hauptkommissar Helmut Fischer', I assumed equivalent to our Chief Inspector. The photo was clearly the fellow in front of me.

"Now that we've met, let's go outside," he said. "There's a waiter around if you want a drink."

As Fischer led the way, I gave him a closer look. Not quite the schoolboy I'd first thought; probably late thirties. Nevertheless, young for a senior policeman. Fast-tracking I believe they called it. He was around six-foot tall, dark haired, with a passing resemblance to actor George Clooney. Dressed in an open-neck blue shirt, shorts and solid boots, he looked more like a hiker than a cop.

Fischer chose one of the more secluded tables and I ordered a stein of beer from the waiter.

"Cheers!" He raised his glass.

I responded: "Can I assume from all this that the inquiry into Jonny Kästner's death has moved on?"

He nodded. "From the Land – our word for the individual State – to the Federal. Germany is a Federal Republic, much of its power being derogated to the various Länder…"

"Derogated": I liked that. His English was almost perfect; just a hint of the odd 'w' turning into a 'v'.

But I had to pay attention. He was continuing: "…So naturally, the initial investigation was handled by the Saxony State Police, under Inspector Kirst. However, certain facts have come to light that indicate it should now be a Federal matter."

"What sort of facts?"

He paused, refreshed himself with more beer, then asked: "Have you any idea how many political parties we have in Germany?"

"Half a dozen?"

He smiled. "At present there are seven with seats in the Bundestag. But if you include all the hopefuls trying their luck at the ballot box, I believe the figure last time was thirty-eight."

"A lot."

"A crazy number. Often with crazy politics. We have Anarchists, Trotskyites, bog-standard Leftists, Independence for Bavaria, Neo-Nazis, Party of Punks, Pirates, you name it."

"The lunatic fringe," I said. "Find them in every country. We once had a guy whose hobby was standing for the Monster Raving Loony Party. Never won a seat, but livened up the political landscape."

"Livening up the political landscape is fine as long as it goes no further. But if the crazies start getting their hands on power…" Fischer shook his head.

"I'm guessing your job is to prevent that."

"I work for the anti-extremism branch of the BKA – that's the Bundeskriminalamt – which recent elections are making ever more relevant."

"I seem to remember Angela Merkel had a problem forming a government," I said.

"For about four months Germany was actually *without* a government. The country carried on much as usual, of course, but the legislative process came to a stop, while the politicos argued."

"Wasn't that a temporary glitch?

"Such 'temporary glitches' are quite new and seem set to become worse and more frequent. Ever since the Bundesrepublik was launched after the war as West Germany, two parties have been dominant: The Christian Democrats and the Social Democrats. Something like your Conservatives and Labour. There have been other smaller parties in various coalitions, but the two big beasts have been the CDU and SPD."

"And now the big beasts are getting old and decrepit."

Fischer sighed. "There's always young blood waiting in the wings, ready to take advantage of any weakness at the top."

"And you don't like the look of this young blood?"

"All over the world extremists are on the march. We seem to have more than our fair share. Most of these organisations are little more than a nuisance, but if they manage to break the five percent barrier they can cause trouble…"

"The five percent barrier?"

Fischer nodded. "In our elections we have two votes: one for a constituency candidate, another for the party. The idea being that if a party wins, say, thirty percent of the vote, it should end up with about thirty percent of Bundestag seats."

"Unlike in Britain, where the two are often miles apart."

Fischer smiled. "*You* said it. The British system is heavily weighted in favour of the establishment parties; and almost impossible for any upstarts. In all fairness, your UKIP should have got over sixty seats instead of just one."

"Where does your five percent barrier come in?"

"The party vote is our way of balancing the books, so that the number of seats won does reflect the number of votes cast. This means some complicated juggling, because almost all the constituency seats will go to the two big beasts. To redress the balance, most of the party votes have to go to everyone else…"

He paused and grinned. "…Are you with me?"

"I think so."

"It's the way we deal with this big block of votes – well over half the Bundestag seats – that's important. We could do like the Israelis and allocate seats strictly according to the numbers, so one percent of the vote earns one percent of the seats. This is very fair and very impractical, because you end up with a mass of tiny parties. Fragmentation. Chaos. So our Constitution sets a threshold, below which you get nothing. Zilch."

"The five percent barrier!" I said triumphantly.

"Exactly! A four point nine percent vote gets you nothing. Five point one percent and you're in business."

"And you're afraid extremist parties may hit the five percent?"

"One of them already has. Alternative for Germany went from under five percent, therefore zero seats, to ninety-four seats. Overnight. AfD insists it's not that extreme, but it scares the hell out of the establishment."

"I gather Jonny Kästner ran an outfit that was even more extreme than the AfD."

Fischer nodded. "Jonny was leader of the German Democratic Right, which in German acronyms comes out rather neatly as the DDR."

"Same letters as the former East Germany."

Fischer nodded. "Deliberate, of course. You must understand, Mr. Blake, that in this part of the country there's still some nostalgia for the old days."

"For Communism? You must be joking."

"Indeed, I'm not. As someone born and bred in the West – I come from Frankfurt, the one on the Main, not the Oder – I, too, find this difficult to understand. For me, Stasiland was an inefficient and corrupt police state, with nothing to recommend it. But many people here see things differently. In those days everyone had a job, usually an undemanding one. With virtually no competition, stress levels were low. Above all, the place was almost totally free of foreigners. Germany for Germans. It's no accident that we're now sitting in the heartlands of this new ultra-right party, the AfD. In the country overall they polled over twelve percent, which is scary enough. Here in Saxony they polled a massive twenty-seven percent."

"Wow!"

"Wow indeed. In former Stasiland over a quarter of voters want to kick out foreigners and be featherbedded by the State."

"All very interesting," I said. "But what's this got to do with Jonny Kästner; who's now dead and can do no more damage?"

"We don't like gang warfare on our streets – or, for that matter, on our rivers. Reminds us too much of the Twenties and Thirties when killings were daily events."

"Those were chaotic times," I said. "Quite different to the peaceful and stable Germany of today."

"Exactly. It's my job to make sure Germany remains peaceful and stable, which isn't a given."

"You think Jonny was killed by a rival gang – a rival party?"

"Either that or by someone *within* his own DDR."

"Surely not?"

"Revolutionary politics has always been a deadly affair, murder not restricted to the ranks of the official enemy. During Weimar days the streets of Germany ran with blood as the two rival ideologies, Nazis and Communists, fought it out. Then, almost as soon as Hitler became Chancellor, he had his oldest buddy, Ernst Röhm, shot and his army of followers purged. The same happened in the Communist homeland, where Stalin killed millions of his own people. A collective madness."

"Whether Jonny was killed by one of his own or by someone from the opposition, I don't understand why you want to talk to *me*," I said. "You surely don't believe Feldmann's ridiculous story? I can't still be a suspect, can I?"

"Inspector Kirst and I both agree you're no longer in the frame as the killer. No motive. Not the type. However, I have to start somewhere. And that somewhere is the last person to have seen Jonny Kästner alive. You."

I had a sudden thought: "I still don't know how he was killed."

"A sharp instrument, probably the sort of knife to be found in every kitchen."

"It wasn't in the body?"

Fischer shook his head. "Nor in the boat, in spite of a thorough search. Must have been thrown overboard. If my department had limitless resources and time, I could perhaps order a team of divers into the Elbe, but even if we found the weapon, it's unlikely to yield much useful information."

"Might the killer have blood on his clothes?" I suggested.

"If he had, everything will by now be cleaned up. Anyway, it looks as though the whole incident happened too fast for much blood to be left on the attacker. The autopsy shows that the weapon entered at abdomen level and was driven up into the heart. Efficiently done. Just a few seconds to then tip Kästner into the engine compartment, get rid of the knife and disappear."

"No one saw anything?"

"What were *you* doing during the steamer's cruise?"

"Admiring the scenery."

"Exactly. Looking the other way. The engine and paddles would have drowned out any noise the execution might have generated."

"Then, to really make your day, all possible suspects disappear into thin air," I said, perhaps tactlessly.

Fischer did not take my comment amiss; merely nodded and said: "It's an interesting investigation."

The Chief Inspector drank up his beer and got to his feet: "I have a suggestion, Mr. Blake. An invitation. You may have noticed I'm scarcely dressed for police work, more a vacation. That's because I find business is more productive if there's also an element of pleasure. Do you have any plans for dinner tonight?"

I shook my head.

"Excellent. Because I've booked a table for two at the Restaurant am Fluss. I can recommend their blue trout. There we can watch the river go by and have, I hope, an interesting discussion."

I inclined my head. "Accepted. With pleasure."

"I need a shower and change of clothes, so shall we say another fifteen minutes?"

"Are you also staying here?"

Fischer smiled. "Of course. Best place in town."

The Chief Inspector disappeared into the hotel, taking the stairs two at a time. I followed at a more leisurely tempo.

Eight

The Restaurant am Fluss lay on the banks of the river Elbe. It was just as well we had reserved a table, because it was a warm evening and we got the last place on the outside terrace. Over to our right was the grassy slope where it had all started with an impromptu football match with Jonny and his boy. The river, slow and placid, was behaving itself, which was not always the case according to the high water marks on the establishment's front door: clients turning up on 16th August 2002 would have had to dine in their scuba gear.

Chief Inspector Fischer had been transformed from a hiker into something of a dandy: neatly pressed fawn trousers, clean new blue shirt, polished brown shoes. This was a George Clooney lookalike, out to impress the ladies, except he only had me for company. Again, I wondered what all this was about.

Until orders had been placed we made inconsequential chat. When full wine glasses were safely on the table I said:

"I find it difficult to believe that your interest in me is simply because, in your words, you have to start somewhere. Or that I was the last person to see Jonny alive."

Fischer smiled. "Maybe I was being slightly devious. But you're an interesting man, Mr.… er… as we're being informal, do you mind if I call you Ed?"

"Not at all…" as *he* had suggested it: "…Helmut."

He grinned. "Just for this evening, you understand. Wouldn't do in a formal interview."

"Of course not. But you're wrong in thinking I'm interesting. My friends consider me rather boring."

"Maybe 'unusual' is a better word. We don't find many middle-aged men driving around Europe on their own."

"I'm recently divorced. With time on my hands."

He nodded. "Your ex-wife, Margaret, receives a generous settlement, but that's hardly left you penniless. You have a daughter, Jane, recently qualified as a doctor. And a son, Jeremy, doing well for himself in the City. Both children off your hands. After a successful career, you now have both the time and resources for a holiday. But why choose Germany? Why not the Caribbean?"

"Wrong season for the Caribbean. And I happen to think Germany is Europe's most under-rated tourist country; has everything except reliable weather and even that's been behaving itself."

"And you already know the country well from your business days."

"Sounds like you know more about me than I do."

He smiled. "Information is everything. Always has been, always will be."

"To begin with, my only commercial interests lay in what was then West Germany," I said. "That went pretty well, so one day I had this crazy idea: why not see what the guys the other side of the Iron Curtain were up to? Try my luck in the DDR; that's the former East Germany, not Jonny Kästner's party."

"Did you find much business in the DDR?"

"You must be kidding! Although I'd been encouraged by their much-publicised Leipzig Trade Fair, in practice I found 'trade' to be a dirty word under Karl Marx. My trip was a financial non-event. But otherwise fascinating. Once I had the necessary paperwork and was over the border, I could do much as I liked. Drive anywhere; talk to anyone. With not a sign of the dreaded Stasi. It was all rather... genteel... sleepy. As I imagined life might have been in the old Austro-Hungarian Empire."

"Sleepy was right," confirmed Helmut. "Which is why it's been so difficult bringing the old DDR into the market-orientated west. When we first took a proper look at our brethren in the east, we were appalled. The autobahns had been the wonder of the world when they'd been built in the Thirties, but no one had touched them in nearly sixty years. If a bridge had crumbled, they didn't bother with anything silly like repairs, but simply coned off the dangerous part and went from two lanes to one. It was a nation of spectacular neglect."

"My favourite vignette of East Germany was when I was trying to find the centre of Weimar," I said. "Signposting was one of their many weak points, so I missed downtown completely. However, I'd spotted a promising place on the way in; something going on behind a high wall, maybe an historic building. Before going in, I thought it best to check with one of the waiting taxis, which was just as well, because this hive of activity turned out to be... the crematorium. The most lively business in Communist Weimar was death."

Helmut smiled: "That's the mindset we've been trying to change these past decades. On the whole we've been quite successful; our eastern city centres now as good as anything in the west. But behind these fancy facades it's another matter. Drop me into any town in Germany, and within two minutes I'll be able to tell you whether it had been in the east or the west. The peeling walls… untended areas… the signs are still there."

"Even now, work in progress," I said.

He nodded. "Not only in the physical sense. It's also in the mind. Here they still think and behave differently."

"Is that why extremist organisations like Jonny Kästner's DDR do so well here?"

"It can't be just a coincidence."

"Well, that's your problem, Helmut. Not mine. But sitting here enjoying a lovely view, some excellent wine and a tasty blue trout, I have a nasty feeling you want me to share in some of those problems."

Fischer said: "Inspector Kirst was most complimentary about your German."

"Which is not in the same league as your English."

"That's because English is our second language. Some firms even use it in their boardrooms."

"What's my scrappy German got to do with the death of Jonny?"

"As you'll have gathered, we have no leads on who might have killed him," replied Fischer.

"Because you have no idea who was aboard the Kurort Rathen."

He nodded. "Unlike planes, Elbe steamers don't require any form of ID to buy a ticket. And because Kirst thought he had the case sewn up, he looked no further than you. However, we've not been idle. Checks have been under way on Kästner's family and associates. Including his wife, Josie."

"Who, I'm told, lives just around the corner from here," I said. "With their son Karl, my young football fan."

"Now also with a fellow called Werner Breitling."

"A replacement for husband Jonny?"

"All we know is that when Jonny left for Dresden about six months ago, Breitling moved in with Josie, even though the Kästners remain legally married. This appears to have been less a domestic squabble than political infighting."

"You mean they're all members of this shadowy German Democratic Right."

Fischer nodded. "These organisations are difficult to come to grips with, but all three of them – Jonny, Josie and Werner – are party members. Although Jonny was the official leader, it appears there had recently been something of a power struggle."

"A reason to kill Jonny?"

"Who knows? It's a line of enquiry we're pursuing."

Suddenly I saw were all this was leading. Held up my hands. Said: "No, no! Nein! Niemals! In whatever language you like."

Fischer smiled smugly. "I don't know what you mean."

He knew perfectly well, but I spelt it out: "I'm being wined and dined because you want me to help crack the puzzle of Jonny Kästner and his goddam political ambitions."

"It happens that you're in a particularly advantageous position…" he began.

I cut him short: "No way! I'm on holiday. Through no fault of my own, I've been caught up in some of your skulduggery. But I'm in the clear. As you've admitted. So I'll be on my way, if don't mind. Even if you *do* mind."

Fischer didn't bat an eyelid. My outburst over, he continued: "I believe Inspector Kirst has asked you to remain in the area for the time being."

"Only until my position has been clarified. Which it now has."

"That may be your view, but it's not Inspector Kirst's."

"But… you've already said…" I didn't like the way this conversation was going.

"We may consider your direct involvement unlikely, but the fact is you were the first person at the scene of the crime. And many questions remain unanswered."

"Inspector Kirst's a silly old fool!" As soon as the words were out of my mouth, I regretted them.

"Inspector Kirst is an extremely able policeman with vast experience – many more years in the job than me, I might say. He will be dealing with the actual killing, while I concentrate on the political angle, but this investigation is a combined operation. With a lot of overlap. If Inspector Kirst says 'Jump!', you jump. Or, in this case, you stay. Until he tells you otherwise."

"I'm sorry," I said. If anyone had been a 'silly old fool' it had been me. "Don't know what came over me."

"Don't worry. People often react like this." Fischer was refilling my wine glass. "Stress. Say things you don't mean. Looking on the bright side, you'll be able to see more of Trudi Lindtner. Who, I believe, has offered to keep you busy while you wait."

I had forgotten Trudi. Perhaps the outlook was not so bleak, after all. Starting to be resigned to my fate, I asked:

"What do you want me to do?"

"We recovered a mobile phone from Jonny's body," replied Fischer. "Our experts have gone through it for all useful information and now we need to return it to his next of kin: his wife, Josie. That could be your job."

"Why me?"

"You could be our conduit into the murky world of the DDR and German extremist politics."

"How do I explain having the phone?"

"He gave it to you. Or he dropped it and you picked it up. You were the last person to have any contact with him. Use your imagination."

44

I shook my head helplessly. Shady stuff like this had never been my forte.

"You have another advantage," continued Fischer remorselessly. "Your friendship with young Karl. The lad has obviously taken a shine to you, so play on it. Josie may well welcome someone like you at this difficult time."

"Then what?"

"Play it by ear. Try and find out what Josie Kästner and her boyfriend Werner Breitling are up to. What makes the German Democratic Right Party, the DDR, tick. Anything that might be of interest to the anti-extremism desk of the BKA. This case has two aspects: the murder of Jonny Kästner and the political dangers of the extreme Right. The two may be linked. Or they may not. Either way, we'd like to know."

"What if I say no? Decide to go home. You've admitted I'm innocent."

Fischer grinned. A nasty grin. "At present the media are frantically trying to work out what happened. The body of a local politician is found stabbed in an old paddle steamer, with no clues as to who dunnit. Headline stuff. So far you've been lucky. By a quirk of fate you were the last to leave the boat, so only the police were around when Feldmann made his ill-advised accusation. Had you been disembarking with the crowd, Feldmann's shout would have instantly brought half a dozen smartphones to bear. Your face would now be on every front page and TV screen."

"But I'm innocent," I complained.

Another unpleasant grin from Fischer: "That's as maybe. But I can just see the headlines: not only here, also back in England. *The Sun*, *Mirror*, *Mail*, every tabloid. 'British man interviewed by German police over brutal paddle steamer killing'. Shouldn't wonder if they didn't also mention paedophilia."

"But I'm innocent," I wailed.

"What's that got to do with it? They'd only be reporting the facts. That you have indeed been questioned by us. Not arrested or charged, merely helping us with our enquiries, as they say."

"Therefore innocent," I said for the third time. The denial didn't convince even me.

Fischer spelt it out starkly: "It's called trial by media. Deplorable, but happens all the time. People would soon be saying 'no smoke without fire'. The public would love it."

"Maggie bloody would!" I muttered grimly.

"Of course, all this need never happen," said Fischer.

"I thought you said…?"

"I said so far you'd been lucky. Because no one has as yet been able to put a name to the mysterious person who was reportedly driven to Dresden police station. For obvious reasons, Inspector Kirst is anxious to play the whole thing down; has been fobbing everyone off with platitudes. I'm happy to do the same…" The Chief Inspector paused to refresh himself with more wine. "… As long as I'm able to pursue the necessary lines of enquiry. However, if my investigations become blocked in any way… it's an unfortunate fact that leaks do sometimes occur."

"You wouldn't…!" At the last moment I realised it would be foolish to use the word 'blackmail'.

Fischer smiled sweetly. "I certainly would. But look on this as an unanticipated adventure. Accompanied, if you so wish, by Frau Lindtner. But be warned: Trudi is something of a gossip, so if you want to stop your little secret becoming *un*-secret, you should lose no time swearing her to silence."

"I was planning to see a bit of the Czech Republic, Slovakia, Hungary, Poland. How long before I'll be back on the road?"

"No idea," replied Fischer airily. "As long as it takes. First thing is to establish yourself with the widow Kästner. See how it goes from there."

"In return for which you'll make sure no one discovers my name?"

"Reporters are devious and unpleasant creatures, so I can give no absolute assurances. I'll only say that if your name does appear, it won't be our fault."

In my business life I'd learnt to be flexible. Not every pet scheme had come to fruition. If one avenue closed, I'd look for another. Helmut Fischer was right. Becoming an unofficial, temporary and unpaid member of the German police might not be such a bad idea after all. Could even be fun. Anyway, I had little option. So I raised my glass:

"To my success with the widow Kästner."

Helmut clinked my glass: "Remember the two aces you hold: your friendship with young Karl and this, Kästner's mobile." He handed me a slim mobile, which I accepted as though it were a grenade.

We finished our meal on subjects unrelated to crime. I went to bed determined to enjoy my new role.

Nine

Next morning, as soon as I'd finished breakfast, I went hunting for Trudi Lindtner, to stop her telling everyone about that guest who'd been accused of the Kästner killing. No doubt I was naïve, but it was only when Fischer had spelt out the awful media possibilities that I'd realised Ed Blake might become a household name. Not the end of the world, but my reputation would forever have a question mark against it.

I found Trudi busy with hotel work, but prepared to give me a few moments of her time. To my relief, she assured me she wouldn't dream of telling anyone. But offered to do anything to help.

"There might be one thing…" I began hesitantly.

"Yes?"

"Chief Inspector Fischer wants me to contact Frau Kästner. A lady I've never met. You know what usually happens to cold calls…"

"Cut off in your prime," Trudi grinned. "So you'd like me to do the phoning. Break the ice?"

"I'd be most grateful. You may not be best friends, but around here everyone knows the Hotel Lindtner. And its owner."

"No time like the present." Trudi marched briskly towards the nearest landline, which happened to be on the reception desk, consulted a list and punched in some numbers.

Frau Lindtner was *not* cut off in her prime. In fact, the person at the other end – was it Josie Kästner? – seemed quite interested.

"Yes, he tells me he has Jonny's phone…" Trudi gave me a wink. "No, I *don't* know how he got it… Says he was playing football with Jonny and your son… Yes, *that* man… He's prepared to deliver it to you in person, so… That's right… Any time today…? I'll let him know where to find you."

"Frau Kästner is very keen to have her phone back," said Trudi, as she replaced the receiver. "Couldn't understand how you came to have it."

"Heard you say she'd be in all day. Doesn't she have a job?"

Trudi shrugged. "They say Josie Kästner is the one who actually runs the DDR. A job in itself, but apparently done from her own home. Pop along and find out."

"I'll do that. And thanks for the phone call. Before I go I should tell you I'm under a sort of loose Saxony arrest; must not leave the area until they give me the okay. Which means I can't check out for a while. You said you could use some more manpower…?"

Trudi grinned. "You don't look the chambermaid type, so I'll excuse changing the bed linen. But I could do with a handyman. There's a broken curtain rail in room thirty-seven. And some of the patio tiles need re-seating – don't want to be sued for a broken ankle. I also need someone on a more regular basis. Panic hours are from around six in the evening until after dinner. Could you commit yourself to this sort of schedule?"

I don't like loafing, so if I *had to* hang around Die Stadt I'd prefer to be kept busy. I saw no reason why my efforts to ingratiate myself with Josie Kästner could not be done during the day, leaving evenings free for Trudi and her hotel.

I replied: "I can't give you a one hundred per cent guarantee. Fischer has first claim on my time and I've no idea how any meetings with Frau Kästner will pan out. But having a job would be a good excuse for staying in the area. So yes. I'm ready to give it a go."

Trudi Lindtner enveloped me in a hug. A kiss on both cheeks. She stood back, wiped the lipstick marks from my face and said: "Welcome to the team."

Recovering my poise, I asked: "What exactly will be my duties during that evening slot?"

"Nothing 'exactly' about it. We have a flexi system. Go where you're needed. I like to welcome our guests, check them in, show them to their rooms, pour their first drinks. Which is impossible. Can't be in two places at once. You're a big boy; have run your own business. Do I have to spell it out?"

"Okay, I'll be your number two."

She nodded. "Starting tonight at six. Don't be late."

"No ma'am."

I gave her a mock salute. I could think of worse fates than being Trudi Lindtner's sidekick.

Ten

Now that Josie Kästner knew who I was, I rang back on my own account to arrange a visit; better that way than turning up unannounced. She suggested two o'clock that afternoon, which left the morning free for some of Trudi's little jobs. The curtain rail in room thirty-seven was easily put right, but the patio tiles were not for me: back-breaking stuff and best left to the experts.

Although I had been given directions, it was unclear how far out of town the Kästner house lay, so I took the Porsche rather than walk; just as well, because although not that far as the crow flew, Die Stadt was backed by a plateau, about 300ft higher up, which could only be reached by a series of hairpins. A good mile by road and quite a climb.

The Kästners lived in a modest house, one of a pair, set just off the road. I parked beside a blue Dacia, made in Romania and therefore popular in Communist days, when the waiting time for them had been about five years; worth it then, because they were reckoned to be better than the home-grown Trabbies. Quality was now greatly improved, but Kästner's Dacia must have been at least a dozen years old, had a broken near-side wing mirror and looked dusty and bedraggled. Rather like the rest of the property.

As I killed the engine, the front door opened to reveal an apparition. No, I'm being unfair. This was just the reaction of a dinosaur – me, unable to appreciate modern trends. Hair dyed a sort of mauve-red is no doubt attractive, although it could have done with a re-spray because the roots were starting to show the original black; events of the past few days had been enough to push personal appearance well down the list of things to do. A jewel piercing the lower lip and some tattoos on her arms completed the picture.

She shook my hand, said: "Come inside. Coffee's on the go."

He voice was slightly croaky, again maybe the result of recent traumas. She was very small, not merely in height – barely five foot – but also in build, which was almost boyish. She was wearing a long, multi-coloured skirt, which looked as though it might have started life as a peasant costume for some amateur dramatics.

Josie Kästner's kitchen-living room was light and airy. It just avoided being slovenly; messy, certainly, but seemed clean. My attention was quickly captured by the other person in the room: Karl.

"How's the brave boy?" I asked.

It was an attempt to lighten the mood, because he looked far from brave. In fact, both of them looked awful; the result of living the nightmare.

"He should be at school," explained Josie. "But they thought it best if he stayed at home until the fuss dies down. Kids can be pretty cruel to each other."

"The fuss is already dying down," I assured her. "Yesterday the Lindtner was packed; almost a beds-in-broom-cupboards situation. Every reporter in the country in town for the big story. But the media's attention span is about thirty seconds and today we're almost back to normal. Like to get back to school, eh Karl?"

The boy nodded, without enthusiasm.

"He was very close to Jonny," explained Josie. "So he's taking it hard."

"As I'm sure you are." My comment wasn't entirely designed to boost her confidence; it was also an attempt to probe her feelings towards Jonny.

She poured the coffee, asked if I took milk or sugar, then said: "Jonny had been gone over six months. I was getting used to him not being here."

I chanced the most impertinent question: "But I believe you *do have* company?"

She nodded. "Werner. He spends most of the day at headquarters, running the show with our members…"

"DDR members?"

She nodded. "When the office closes, he comes here with all the paperwork to process… then often sleeps over."

"I believe Jonny was the party leader," I said.

For the first time she tried a smile. "Everyone loved Jonny. He was almost *too* nice."

Another impertinent question: "Why did he move out?"

She shook her head, as though trying to erase the memory: "You know what politics is like…"

I had no idea what politics was like, so I asked: "Argumentative?"

A grim smile: "That would be a nice way of putting it. Jonny and Werner were forever at daggers drawn."

"But why did Jonny, your husband, feel he had to leave home? And let Werner in?"

"Jonny was always the poster boy. The acceptable face of our movement. He felt he had to be nearer the centre of things. In Dresden. Where people could see him. Meet him. Not out here in the sticks."

"Must have been a terrible blow for the party when he was killed."

Josie looked at me as though I were mad. Shook her head. Said: "You obviously don't understand."

I could think of nothing to say. She was right. I didn't understand.

"That's the reason *he* had to die," she explained. "Had it been Werner, me, any of the others, no one would have taken much notice. But when our pin-up boy is murdered, well… just look:

"MARTYRED". The heavy type screamed out from a news sheet she handed me. It was headed *DDR News*.

I read on:

"Yesterday Johann Kästner, founder and inspirational leader of the German Democratic Right, was callously murdered. The police know the killer must be one of the millions of foreigners who have invaded our country. And are now killing our men. Yet no arrests have been made. How much longer will we have to tolerate this poison?" And so on, in similar vein.

I could see what Josie meant. There was nothing like a martyr to gee up the troops and make them hopping mad. Jonny's death was most convenient for the DDR.

So I asked: "Do *you* think Jonny was killed by one of these… foreign invaders?"

She shrugged. "It's possible."

"If not?"

"Werner was at a meeting in Dresden, with a dozen others. So it can't have been him. And, in spite of everything, *I* still loved Jonny."

That Josie could even contemplate Werner being involved showed how bitter the rivalries must be within the DDR. Her denial I took at face value. It's not unknown for disgruntled wives to kill their spouses, but Josie's grief seemed all too genuine. Anyway, Jonny Kästner's killer must have been on the boat, so Josie – like Werner – had a cast-iron alibi.

Looking at the two of them, both shattered by recent events, I was overcome by a strange feeling. I didn't find Josie in the least attractive. She had not been born a beauty, but that need not have mattered. I could think of many girls, far from raving beauties, who nevertheless had the boys queuing up for them, because they made the most of the hand nature had dealt them. Josie, with her weird ideas of body art and awful dress sense, seemed determined to make the *worst* of God's gifts.

No, Josie Kästner did not turn me on. But I did feel… The best word I can think of is 'protective'. I would have put her age at early thirties, so only a little older than my children. I felt a bit like her father; and Karl's granddad.

How did these feelings square with the fact that she was a leading figure in a most unappetising organisation? One that Helmut Fischer's BKA, the Federal Crime Office, was worried about. One that might have just killed their leader, either for political publicity or in the course of an internal power struggle. The piece she had shown me from the *DDR News* was depressingly similar to the stuff Goebbels had been churning out in the 1930s.

I tried to visualise Josie Kästner a decade or more earlier, in her late teens; idealistic and impressionable, keen to make the world a better place; the time of life when youngsters hitched themselves to 'a cause'. They might work in that cause for years, progress through the ranks, eventually perhaps becoming someone important. A major investment in time and effort.

As every investor knows, if that sure-fire stock you bought years ago turns out to be a turkey, it's horribly difficult to decide whether to bail out, and if so, when. Many people never summon up the courage and go down with the sinking ship. Was Josie still truly wedded to the DDR? Or was she just hanging in there, unable to summon up the courage to quit?

"…I said, do you have Jonny's phone?"

I'd been away with the fairies; hadn't registered that Josie had been asking the question which was the excuse for my visit: the return of Jonny's phone.

"Of course." I delved into a pocket and handed it over.

She took it, unsettled, suspicious: "I don't understand. Why did Jonny give it to *you*?"

I'd given this question a good deal of thought and come up with no satisfactory answer, so had to fall back on the least unsatisfactory: "He didn't give it. I took it. I was the first person on the scene. Jonny, lying there in the engine room. It was horrible. The phone was sticking out of his back pocket. A private thing, a phone. I thought someone close to him should have it. His wife, if there was one…"

I thought Josie was about to question this feeble version of events. Instead, she asked: "Have you had it all the time? Has anyone else seen it?"

I'd also given *this* question much thought. I couldn't tell her the police would have squeezed everything useful out of it. Which left only one option: to lie as convincingly as possible.

I shook my head and replied: "Just me. Had the phone since I took it. Didn't know you existed until your name appeared in the papers. When it did… well, here I am."

I don't know whether Josie believed me. She just grunted and put the phone in her handbag.

Keen to move on from this touchy topic, I said: "Would you like me to take Karl off your hands for a couple of hours?

As he's not at school. We could go for a drive in my car… find somewhere to knock a ball about."

Josie looked dubious, but the lad had no qualms. Anything to get away from the house of death. He was on his feet in an instant:

"Please mum! I'll be good. Promise."

"I've got kids of my own" I said, in case that made any difference. "Although they're grown up now. Karl reminds me of my son a few years back."

Probably out of sheer exhaustion, Josie gave in. Told me not to be late bringing him back. And Karl to behave himself.

The two of us set off, armed with the same football we'd used when Jonny had invited me to join 'Die Stadt United'. We drove around for a while; found a meadow where we could bash the ball around. I kept the conversation casual, away from anything that might stir memories. We discussed the top teams in the English Premiership, German Bundesliga, Italian Serie A. Two lads together. Stayed well clear of all painful subjects.

Mindful of my new obligations at the Hotel Lindtner, I delivered Karl back at five-thirty to find there was now another car in the Kästner drive: a black Toyota that was classier, newer and cleaner than Josie's Dacia.

"Uncle Werner's," explained Karl, as we stopped.

The front door opened before we even got out. He was built like a brick shithouse, a tree-trunk neck merging into a bull head, shaved on top and a few days of designer stubble below. He was wearing dark shorts and a sleeveless tunic, for biceps display. He looked the sort of man who would usually favour a gallery of body art, but, unlike his girlfriend, was devoid of visible tattoos. Uncluttered skin, muscle-bound and menacing.

"You shouldn't go out with strange men," he said, as Karl scuttled past him towards the safety of his mother.

"My fault," I said. "Karl and I are old pals. He needed a change of scene; fresh air and some exercise."

"*We* decide what the boy needs."

Werner did not offer me coffee. Did not invite me in. Shut the door in my face.

Eleven

I enjoyed my inaugural evening as the Hotel Lindtner's general factotum. Trudi liked to greet her guests, chat them up, make her mark. As there was often a check-in queue, my role became that of the bellboy, humping their bags up to the third floor, there being no lifts. The hotel described itself as 'traditional', but I saw no reason why that should exclude modern contrivances to get you up from ground level. Maybe it was another example of the way Germany's eastern provinces, the former DDR, still lagged behind the west.

When the check-in rush subsided, I found myself transformed into a barman; and when dinner was in full swing a sommelier. It was fun, if hectic.

It was after eleven before we could draw breath. With her customers now well fed and wined, Trudi could finally sit down. In a replay of the previous evening, she invited me into the empty dining room and locked the door from the inside.

Fetched a bottle of white wine, poured a glass for both of us and asked:

"How did you get on with Josie Kästner?"

I told her, adding: "I felt sorry for her. She may be a hippy type working for a nasty outfit, but came over as, well… rather pathetic."

"Having to organise her husband's funeral can't help."

"What was Jonny Kästner really like?" I asked. "Even though he'd abandoned Josie, she said she still loved him. Said *everyone* loved him."

"Every politician busts a gut to get themselves loved, but few succeeded as well as Jonny Kästner. Never met him, but by all accounts he was a great guy. Must mean something if his discarded wife still holds a torch for him."

"Unlike the current boyfriend, who was most unlovable; at least to me."

"I don't know much about Werner Breitling," admitted Trudi. "He comes from somewhere the other side of Dresden; Meissen, I think. The Kästners are a local family and although I'm not in their circle, I keep up with the gossip."

"So…" I took a sip of wine. "That sums up the Kästners. It's not a lot, but more than I know about my new employer."

She seemed pleased to be asked, but also embarrassed: "I'm just a simple country girl, trying to earn an honest pfennig."

"Always lived here?"

She nodded. "Born and bred. Very boring."

"So you'll have grown up under the old regime." I avoided the word 'Communist'.

"Of course. When the wall came down, I was… older than you might think."

I was too much of a gentleman to probe further into her age, so just asked: "What was it like? Before the Wall came down?"

"Nice and peaceful, actually. Less hectic. Certainly less materialistic."

"Did you prefer it that way?"

She gave the question some thought. Finally replied: "It was *different*. Now it's more interesting. Whether that's always a good thing…" She shrugged.

"What did you do? In those days?"

"You ask a lot of questions."

"I'm sorry. Just curious." Maybe I'd gone too far.

"No, no, it's good to talk. But if we carry on like this, I need something stronger."

She went over to a cupboard; came back with two small glasses and a bottle containing a dark liquid.

"Fancy some?"

The label said 'Jägermeister'. A herb digestif. With more of a kick in it than wine. If Trudi felt she needed bolstering, that probably made two of us. I nodded acceptance and she poured for us both.

"In those days, as you put it, I was married," she began. "Franz was seventeen years older than me. Worked for the government."

She said no more. Just sat there looking at me. Pensive. Amused. And damned attractive.

"So?"

"You're not stupid. Work it out."

"Your husband was a government official…" Slowly, the cogs in my brain clicked into place. "You mean…?"

Now she was grinning. "Yes, Franz worked for the Stasi."

"Can hardly blame *you* for that."

"And I was a member of the FDJ, the Free German Youth."

"Sounds harmless enough."

"The FDJ's job was to make sure every youngster had a good 'Socialist Personality'. It was the teenage arm of the party.

I was *very* keen, one of the leaders. Which is how I caught Franz's eye. Naturally I was flattered when one of the bosses started taking an interest in me."

"You were a Stasi couple?"

"You could say that. We were proud of the country which the world knew as East Germany. Punched above our weight in sports; always came back with tons of medals; had a thriving arts and music scene. No one had much money, but neither was anyone really poor. We all had a job. May sound strange now, but many of us felt we had a way of life worth preserving."

"What happened to your husband?"

"He died. In the late nineties. A few years after his country expired. He was a sixty fags a day man, smoked himself to death. But he also lost the will to live. When the wall came down he went from being someone important to an outcast."

"But you adapted."

"As one does at that age. Remember, Franz was almost old enough to have been my father. For me, it helped that he was a Lindtner, a family that had been quite well off before the war. After reunification, most government property was returned to its original owners. As Franz's widow, I found myself with this hotel."

"You've done well. Even though you've had to work harder than in the old days."

Trudi took a sip of Jägermeister. "Can't complain."

"You never married again?"

She shook her head. "Somehow it never happened. Been too busy. Which reminds me…" a mischievous smile… "I have some bad news."

"I'm to be fired? My work been unsatisfactory?"

"Far from it. They love you. Especially that quaint accent. But we have an influx of guests tomorrow. Some sort of cyclathon is using the town as a night stop, so every nook and cranny has been booked. We'll be needing that attic room of yours, so… sorry and all that, but I'll have to throw you out."

She was trying to look stern, but failing. This had to be some sort of a game. Whatever that game might be, I was expected to join in.

I began: "There must surely be… in a town of this size… with your influence…"

"A bed's no problem," she cut in. "There's one here on the premises. But it's in the servants' quarters."

I was beginning to glimpse what her game might be. But I could be wrong. Had to play it carefully.

I said: "Beggars can't be choosers. Anyway, I seem to be your servant now. So I'll say thanks for the offer. On one condition: that I don't have to share a room with that waiter of yours; a nice enough guy, but not my cup of tea."

"What *would* be your cup of tea."

"I'm rather partial to chambermaids."

"Even previously married, ancient chambermaids?"

"Especially that sort."

"Come on, then. I'll see you to your room."

"I thought the cyclathon wasn't until tomorrow?"

"Don't be a sissy." Trudi Lindtner took my hand, led me through the kitchen. And on to the servants' quarters.

Twelve

The servants in the Hotel Lindtner did not suffer. There was a large living room, with a settee, several soft chairs, and a coffee table with the obligatory illustrated books. On a wall was a widescreen TV; in a corner, a desk complete with computer.

I only came to appreciate all this the next morning, because the chambermaid dragged me straight through into the playroom. Otherwise known as the bedroom. Where, after the usual games, I slept the sleep of the just.

I was woken by an alarm. And some fruity German expletives. A servant's day starts early. Trudi staggered up and went to the bathroom. I heard the sound of running water; not only from the bathroom, but also from outside. The window, which I calculated should be beaming in the morning sun, was instead being battered by a newly arrived weather system: welcome news for farmers, not so for holidaymakers.

Trudi returned from the bathroom, half dressed and looking more human. Gave me a peck on the cheek and said:

"That was lovely. There should be a law against girls sleeping alone."

I said: "Josie's party should put a commitment like that into their manifesto. A sure-fire vote winner."

Trudi giggled. "Every bed to be occupied by two persons…"

"Of opposite sex?"

She considered this for a moment, then shook her head. "The people must have a choice. Let's just say it has to be a couple; any mix. Otherwise… well, the guillotine was designed to be the most humane form of execution."

"Joking apart, I don't think I'll be seeing much more of Frau Kästner," I said. "Her bouncer boyfriend won't let me past the front door."

"Is he there all day?"

"Far from it. According to Josie, he almost lives in the party office. Only comes back at night to dump a load of paperwork on her desk. And enjoy his home comforts."

"So you could see Josie when he's not there."

"What would be my excuse? I've delivered Jonny's phone back. Any further visits might be seen as harassment. Or – if I did any more football coaching with young Karl – paedophilia."

Trudi grinned. "Harassment and paedophilia… maybe I *should* throw you onto the street."

"I've done what Fischer asked. Made my mark with Frau Kästner. That business is now concluded. Unless she wants to see more of me, which I doubt."

"So what will you do? Don't tell me I'm back to sleeping alone?"

"Not while this weather lasts." I waved a hand at the rain lashing down. "Even though I've become quite attached to the place – and its wonderful people…" I gave her a kiss. "When the sun comes out again, I'll be ready to go. As soon as Fischer lets me off the leash…"

"When do you think that'll be?"

I shrugged. "I'll have to phone him. Bring him up to date on my visit. But I can't see how he can make me to stay much longer."

Trudi gave me a hug. "Ships that pass in the night. I'll miss you. Not only for the obvious reason, but also because my guests seem to like you. An Englishman serving them. Instead of my usual temporary staff: Poles, Turks, Africans."

"You sound like one of the Kästner's DDR."

She looked embarrassed. "They're too way-out, even for me. But I *did* vote for the AfD."

"You did?" An ex-Stasi activist from the Left supporting the extreme Right? But I shouldn't have been surprised. In politics, the extreme ends of the spectrum have much in common.

"We'll see how it goes," I continued, levering myself into a vertical position. "A shave, breakfast, phone call to Fischer, any jobs madam may inflict on me. This weather looks set for a couple of days, so I should be around for a while."

Thirteen

When I phoned Chief Inspector Fischer he was busy; said he'd ring back in half an hour. I occupied the time moving some of the garden furniture out of the rain; in spite of an accurate weather forecast, the storm had taken everyone by surprise.

When Fischer rang back, he was apologetic. As was his habit, he also spoke in English. I'd become so immersed in German that my own language sounded almost foreign.

I described my visit to Josie Kästner and her boyfriend's rebuff. Asked what he knew about Werner.

"Ah yes, Werner Breitling. The heir apparent."

"He's the DDR's next leader?"

"Not officially. Not yet. Too much of a rush would look bad, so there has to be a period of mourning. But we've now released Jonny Kästner's body and his widow has expressed a wish for cremation. This is less common in Germany than in your country and the nearest crematorium appears to be in

Meissen. The interment is scheduled for Thursday of next week. And the executive of the German Democratic Right is due to meet two days later, on the Saturday, to elect its new leader."

"You reckon Werner will get in?"

"Breitling is the runaway favourite."

"Can't say he impressed me. What do you know about him?"

"Johann Kästner was not only DDR's founder, he was also a charismatic leader. He had a way with the crowds; a knack of making extreme policies sound benign. Breitling is not benign."

"Then why is he on course to be their next leader?"

"He's the Stalin of the DDR. The man who beavers away in head office, almost unnoticed. Didn't Josie say he spent all day, every day there? You don't have to be a leader type to control a political party."

"Josie told me Werner was at a meeting when Kästner was killed," I said. "So he couldn't have been responsible."

"Depends what you mean by 'responsible'. Stalin was never seen with a smoking gun in his hand, but was responsible for more deaths than any other man in history; probably even more than Hitler or Mao."

"You think Werner gave the order to someone else to do the dirty?"

"Seems likely."

"Do you have any leads on who the gunman – or rather the knifeman – might be?"

Fischer's sigh reached me even over the phone: "It was a professional job and – if Werner Breitling was behind it – would have been professionally organised. So far we have nothing."

"Well, I've done what I can. How about lifting your curfew on me? I'd like to be on my way."

"I thought Frau Lindtner might have persuaded you to stay."

I couldn't help laughing. "Have you been bugging her servants' quarters?"

Fischer chuckled. "Intuition. And some knowledge of the good Trudi. A lovely lady. You could do a lot worse."

"Agreed," I said. "But nomadic instinct wins over the boudoir. Besides, I can't see myself spending the summer serving drinks and humping heavy bags up three flights of stairs."

"Could you at least stay on for another couple of days? Until we're sure the Josie Kästner angle is played out."

I looked at the rain, hammering away relentlessly. No point in moving until Central Europe again had some high pressure to offer. So I replied: "Okay, a few more days. Until the sun comes out. When it does, I'll be back demanding release."

Fourteen

I was shifting garden furniture again when my mobile rang. It was Josie. I'd given her my number on the off-chance, not really expecting to hear from her.

"What are you doing right now?" she asked.

"Getting wet."

"Here it's dry. And coffee's ready."

"What about Werner?"

"At the office. Won't be back until much later."

"So?"

"Karl's back at school and I'd like a chat. Seems a good time."

"Coffee and somewhere dry sounds attractive. Be with you in twenty minutes."

I finished the garden furniture job and got into my Porsche. Made it in less than twenty. There was only the blue Dacia in her drive, so no Werner. Just as well to check.

This time Josie welcomed me more as a friend. Knew my coffee habits and poured me a mug. Her amateur dramatics skirt was different and even more amateur. But her crimson hair had been refreshed, the roots now matching. Lip decoration remained the same; more difficult to change? I was no expert.

"Sorry about Werner," she began. "He can be rather rude."

I dismissed his boorish behaviour with a shrug.

She added: "He has a lot on his mind."

I said nothing, so she continued:

"He'll probably be our next leader."

It was on the tip of my tongue to say I'd already heard this from Fischer, then realised I should not be privy to the police investigation. To Josie I was merely an innocent bystander.

Instead, I said: "Congratulations."

"Trouble is, I don't think Werner is cut out for the job."

I was astonished. "Why not? Surely as your boyfriend…?"

"That's the reason. Because I know him better than most. Jonny was brilliant. A people person. Werner is good at what he does, which is crunching numbers, organising the backroom, but…"

She paused, so I filled in: "His charisma is on the heavy side."

She nodded. "He can scare people."

"Scares *everyone*, if the treatment he gave me is anything to go by."

"He means well."

"Are you sure?"

Instead of answering, she said: "When Jonny and I set up the DDR… must be five years ago now, we had *fun*. Of course, we had a serious message – too many immigrants, not enough control over our own destinies – but at the same time we enjoyed ourselves. Then gradually the mood changed…"

Josie withdrew into her own thoughts, so again I ventured an opinion: "Did that change coincide with the arrival of Breitling?"

"No, no. Well, I suppose… I think it was why Jonny left me. Moved to Dresden to be more in control of things. So he could recapture that early flair and optimism."

"While you welcomed the man who was Jonny's problem. Into your own…" I almost said bed. "Into your own house."

She shook her head, as though unable to believe her own actions: "Jonny only came back occasionally, mainly to take Karl out. But Werner I see every day. We're the DDR's backbone. He runs the Dresden office, then every evening brings the day's work here for me to deal with: membership rolls; subscription fees; editing publicity material; all the tedious stuff that keeps our party running. After a while, it seemed pointless for Werner to return every night to Dresden. I was on my own, so…"

"Good of you to tell me all this. You hardly know me."

"That's the reason. You're neutral. Not involved. I need to sound off to *someone*."

"Would you accept some… some observations from that neutral?"

She hesitated briefly, then nodded.

I said: "Werner Breitling seems to antagonise people."

"But he's so clever; so dedicated. We'd be lost without him."

"No one's indispensable. If that person is also a disruptive influence, you should get rid of him."

Josie looked horrified. "We can't do that! He's about to be elected our leader."

"It's not yet a done deed. Elect someone else. Why not stand yourself? As your party's co-founder, I bet you'd get plenty of support."

"I'm not the leader type. Besides, I have Karl to look after."

"Excuses, excuses. Will you at least admit that the party under Werner will be very different from the one you and Jonny gave birth to?"

"Of course. Nothing stays the same. Maybe we need a change."

"Do you really believe that?"

Her silence said it all.

"Who's standing in your leadership election?" I asked.

"Werner, of course. And two others."

"Nonentities, I assume?"

"Wouldn't say that."

"But not you?"

She shook her head. "Even if I'd wanted to, there's too much on my plate at the moment. Jonny's funeral. Then all the money stuff when someone dies…"

She began to snuffle. A handkerchief appeared from a fold in her comic opera skirt.

"I'm sorry… Perhaps I should go…"

"No, no. I wanted to talk." Josie wiped her eyes and gathered herself. "You've been so kind. Specially to Karl."

"If there's anything more I can do…" I began, then, remembering the time element, added: "during the next few days, that is. When the weather clears, I'll be off again."

"You won't be staying?" With all her other problems, the fact that I was merely passing through had evidently not registered.

I replied: "Had it not been for… unusual circumstances, I'd be gone by now."

"I see…" She seemed strangely upset by this news. I'd only been around a few days, so she hardly knew me. Maybe Josie Kästner, in her hour of need, was short of real friends.

So I said: "You have my mobile number. For the next few weeks I'll be the happy wanderer; could easily drift back here to check on things. Anyway, I'd like to see Karl again. Promised to take him see Arsenal play when the football season starts."

She managed a wan smile. "Karl *really* likes you. While he's still at school it's not too bad, but when they break up for the summer…"

I was prepared to do a lot of things, but babysitting Kästner junior during the long summer break was a good deed too far. So I just said: "Let's keep in touch. And remember: the DDR was created by you and Jonny. Make sure it stays true to him."

We nattered on for a few more minutes; finished our coffee. I left with a guilty conscience. Josie Kästner was a sad lady, but what could I do about it?

Fifteen

After dinner that night, Trudi went into what was becoming our routine: told the waiter we would finish clearing the dining room; locked the door; found a newly opened bottle of wine: *and* the Jägermeister. Sat down opposite me and said:

"You had another chat with Josie?"

I nodded. "Not a happy situation. Preparing to bury – or rather, burn – your husband is bad enough. But Werner Breitling is set to be the DDR's next leader and she thinks he'll take the party along a different and more aggressive path than her Jonny."

"The DDR was pretty aggressive under Kästner."

"Well, expect the same only more so. Josie used a strange word when describing the party's early days: said they'd been fun. Whatever Werner might bring, it won't be fun."

"Could lose them a lot of support," said Trudi. "Jonny had a way with him that was… appealing. In politics, the messenger is often more important than the message."

I nodded. "I feel sorry for Josie. A mixed-up girl. She even hinted I might like to take young Karl off her hands for a while during the summer holidays; be a surrogate dad."

"You can't possibly do that!"

"Of course not. It was just a fishing remark and I didn't bite. But it left me feeling bad. Karl and I get on well. On an occasional basis."

"Don't even consider it!"

"I didn't."

"You have your own life to lead…" Trudi took a sip of wine and gave me a little grin. "Which is… what? What are your plans?"

"As before. When the weather clears and your constabulary remove the handcuffs, I'll be off. On my delayed jaunt around Europe."

"Fancy a travelling companion?"

For a moment I didn't get it. Replied off-hand: "An academic question. There isn't anyone."

"Really?" She was at her most winsome.

Then I *did* get it.

"But you're the Hotel Lindtner."

"So you've been canoodling with a load of bricks and mortar? Thought I was more exciting than that."

In an effort to recover some Casanova points, I replied: "You know what I mean. How can you abandon ship in high season?"

"Birgit can take over."

"Birgit?"

"My daughter."

"You never told me you had a daughter."

"There are loads of things I haven't told you."

"How can this… Birgit… up-sticks and take over, just like that?"

"Because she'd like nothing better. At the moment she's supposedly working – in fact, sulking – in a nail bar in Dresden. We're hardly on speaking terms. If I told her she could have the run of our hotel for a while, she'd be on the doorstep faster than the speed of light."

"I don't understand…"

"I don't know what drove you and your wife apart, but some families are war zones. For me to go away for a while might be a chance to repair some of the damage. Build a better future for the business."

"Give your daughter her head? See how she copes?"

Trudi nodded. "The Lindtners go back a long way. To the days when Saxony was part of the Holy Roman Empire. Saxony had one of the Electors who chose those emperors, but in practice it was an independent state. A lot of water has flowed under the Elbe bridges since then: two world wars, then the Stasiland era. Now something like normal service has been resumed and it would be nice to carry on our old traditions: keep the Lindtner name alive, even if through the female line. At least Birgit and I agree on that."

"But she had different ideas on how to run things?"

"Very different. A generational thing. Music, for instance."

"Music?"

"The stuff that goes up and down. Birgit wanted it piped through the hotel. I didn't. I wouldn't have minded some gentle Bach; even Brahms or Beethoven. Good Germans. Give our customers some culture. But Birgit wanted all that American rubbish. Noisy, no tunes. We almost came to blows over it."

"She could be right," I said. "Maybe that's what the youngsters *do* want."

Trudi changed from wine to Jägermeister, said: "Over my dead body! If we'd carried on together, *one* of us would have been laid out stone cold. It wasn't just the music. We argued about everything. So when last year's summer season ended, Birgit went off. By mutual consent."

"You didn't think of stepping down yourself ?"

"Of course I thought about it. But I like to keep busy. The idea of being put out to pasture at my age… selfish maybe, but there you are."

"Now that you see something that might keep you amused, you're prepared to leave the hotel to Birgit?"

"For a while. To see how it goes. That's if you'll have me."

"My dear Trudi, of course I'll have you. Although, I must warn you I have some nasty habits…"

"You don't snore: at least, you haven't so far. I'm prepared to risk other defects."

"When the touring season ends in September, what then?" I was more than happy to have Trudi as a travelling companion, but as for anything more permanent, I hardly knew her. I'd already committed years of my life to one fractious female – didn't want to make the same mistake again.

"We see what happens," replied Trudi. "Enjoy ourselves without making any commitments. Or do *you* already have future plans?"

I shook my head. "The break-up with Maggie was pretty traumatic. I had to get away for a while. Clear my head. Of course I do have some vague ideas, but that's all. So if you agree to no promises on either side… let's do it!"

I got a lovely great hug, spiced with Jägermeister fumes. We grappled for a few seconds.

When we broke, I asked: "How soon can you have Birgit in command?"

"Her job in the nail bar is part time, temporary and paid at slave rates, so she could walk out today. Give her a week here, to get the feel of things again, and…"

"Does she have a boyfriend?"

"I expect so."

"You don't know?"

"I told you, we're not on speaking terms. Birgit's personal life is her own affair. Her choice of men has usually been good, so she shouldn't be with anyone who'll trash the place."

"You're happy to give her a second chance?"

"Happy is too strong a word, but I'll risk it. I don't want to be still running the Lindtner as a wrinkled crone of 102. This is my chance to make the break."

"Come on. We've both had enough to drink. Let's celebrate another way." I took Trudi's hand and led her bedwards.

Sixteen

A week to wait was easily borne when I had the promise of a travelling buddy. I became less fidgety, settled down to being the hotel's barman, bellboy and DIY-man. It helped that the weather remained unsettled; the downpour that had broken the hot spell had moved on, but the extended forecast was no better than sunshine and showers; I might as well make myself useful until the meteorological situation became clearer.

Nevertheless, I soon *did* find myself becoming fidgety. It was all very well doing my bit at the hotel, while I mulled over our coming itinerary, but we were going nowhere until Chief Inspector Fischer gave me the all clear. After three days, I could stand it no longer and phoned him. He was busy, so I left a message. A couple of hours later, his secretary rang back to see if I could meet him the next day. The Kästner case was bringing him back to our part of the world, so he suggested another visit to the Restaurant am Fluss. 12.30 for a working lunch. I said I'd be there.

On this occasion there was no sitting outside to enjoy the passing river traffic. It was spitting with rain and the temperature could not have been much above twenty. Although their dining room had a river view, we found ourselves seated in a far corner, up against some wood panelling and overlooked by a stormy canvas of a Teutonic Monarch of the Glen: a horned colossus glaring down at us imperiously.

As we sat down, I commented: "More business than pleasure today, it seems?" Helmut Fischer was dressed in a smart suit and blue tie; with his square-jawed rugged features, he looked more like a film star than a cop.

He nodded. "I'm based in Berlin, but on my way to see Inspector Kirst to talk about Kästner. You may be able to help us, so fire away."

'Fire away': very good. We were back to Fischer's preferred language, English. But I didn't know what I was supposed to 'fire away' with. So I asked:

"What do you want to know?"

"You've been very good with Josie Kästner. My thanks for keeping us in the loop. What's your summing up? Your impression of her?"

I took a moment to gather my thoughts, before replying: "Josie is a hippy-type. Early thirties, so would have met Jonny in her impressionable late teens or early twenties. Whatever his politics, he was someone people took to. My guess is that Josie fell for Jonny rather than his politics. Came to love the DDR because *he* was that party ."

"Now that he's dead, do you think she's becoming less committed?"

"She's certainly asking herself questions. But she has this new boyfriend: Werner Breitling. The party's next leader."

"A substitute for Kästner?"

"Never. At the moment Josie is shell-shocked and confused, so it's no good trying to work out how this will play out. She appeared to tolerate Jonny going to live in Dresden because it was 'for the cause'. Not for another woman. At least, she's never mentioned anyone else."

Fischer nodded. "We've been digging and haven't found another woman either."

"With Jonny away, except for brief visits to see their son, her man about the house became Werner," I continued. "Who arrived every evening with the excuse he had a mass of office work for her to tackle. Because Josie is the sort of girl who needs a man in her bed, Werner soon replaced the party leader in her affections…"

I paused for a correction: "No, no. I shouldn't use the words 'Breitling' and 'affection' in the same breath. Josie respects Werner for his political skills and work ethic; is also probably more than a little scared of him…"

"With good reason," said Fischer grimly. "Breitling's a thug…"

"But affection for Werner? No," I concluded. "He fulfils a physical need and will soon lead the party she helped to found. How she'll come to terms with that, I've no idea."

"Does she think the DDR will change direction?"

"More a change of emphasis than direction. The DDR will become more aggressive. Not good news for you."

"I'm afraid you're right. And it confirms the feedback we've been getting from other sources."

"Have those 'other sources' given you any clues as to who might have killed Jonny Kästner?" I asked.

"We have a working hypothesis. Nothing we can act on."

"And…?" I prompted, when Fischer seemed reluctant to go any further.

"It's only a theory. But you remember the man who accused you?"

"You mean Beer-Gut?"

Fischer cracked a smile. "He's on our records as Josef Feldmann, usually known as Sepp. The man who said he'd heard you confess to the killing."

"Beer-Gut as the culprit would make sense," I mused. "Being a crew member, he would have had a good opportunity to kill Kästner. And when he found me, frozen in terror over his handiwork, he could throw the blame on someone else. It worked a treat. But what about motive?"

"Feldmann is an enthusiastic member of the DDR, often seen around head office. If we accept the theory that Kästner's death was the result of a party leadership struggle, Feldmann could have been Breitling's hit-man. But we can't hold a man on guesswork."

"So you're stuck. With vague theories, but no proof."

"Unfortunately, yes. The Kästner case stays open, but we wind down our work on it. Deploy our resources elsewhere."

"Not very satisfactory."

Fischer sighed. "Much police work is unsatisfactory. We don't live in an Agatha Christie world, with Poirot-like dénouements to explain every puzzle."

"Do I gather from all this that I'm now free to go?"

"As far as I'm concerned, yes. I'll be seeing Inspector Kirst shortly and will also need his okay, but that should be a formality."

"That's a relief."

"Will you be resuming your tour through Europe?"

"Of course. And," I found myself blushing, "Trudi Lindtner will be coming with me."

"That was quick work." The Chief Inspector grinned, then continued: "I have one request: that you keep your mobile phone active and check it from time to time. You seem to have struck up a rapport with Josie Kästner, so we might need your help with her again."

Keeping a listening watch was a small price to pay, so I readily agreed.

"Any idea which countries you'll be visiting?" he asked.

"Depends on the weather. If it stays unsettled over central Europe, I'll probably look for something better down south in the Balkans. But given half a chance, I'd prefer to keep going east. To Poland, Hungary and Romania."

"Summer on the road with your lady. Sounds idyllic," said Fischer wistfully. "Could you also keep a watching brief for me? Extremist groups are on the march all over Europe. Although I keep in touch with colleagues in other countries, there's nothing like reports from people on the ground. Hungary, for example, is almost off the political chart to the right."

"If we come across anything, I'll let you know."

It was said casually. Without a thought. Foolish of me.

Seventeen

Birgit was blonde, like her mother, but slightly taller and two decades more modern in dress. She didn't arrive at the forecast speed of light, because her VW Polo couldn't go that fast. But she didn't hang about either and was clearly in a mood to do business.

I'd read Trudi the riot act: any further family falling-outs were strictly forbidden. The hotel was now her daughter's domain, her own duty to remain schtum. She'd promised to behave.

No boyfriend was visible and we didn't enquire after one. Our role was to keep a low profile, do our bit and watch, while the new boss swung into action. Birgit knew most of the staff from the previous season and seemed to get on well with them. As far as I could judge, the hotel would be in capable hands.

We gave Birgit the one week that had been Trudi's estimate of how long she would need to settle into the saddle again.

Meanwhile, I lost no time in planning to get *our* show on the road. I wanted to be gone before Trudi's small store of patience was exhausted and the Lindtners resumed open warfare.

The day before we were due to leave I gave Josie Kästner a call. Jonny's funeral had taken place a couple of days earlier, so there should now be some sort of closure. Time to look to the future. She had seemed vulnerable and uncertain. I wanted to see how she was coping and maybe inject a bit of cheer and optimism.

Josie suggested I came for 3pm; usually tea and cakes time, although I didn't think she was a cakes person. As it was safely before Werner time, I agreed.

When I drove up, only the battered blue Dacia was visible. Therefore no Breitling. Couldn't be too careful. The later schedule was explained when Josie opened the door and out rushed Karl, back from school.

I greeted him with "Hi there, big boy!"

I was embarrassed when the lad flung himself into my arms. He hadn't done that before. But he had just lost his dad; and his mum's boyfriend was not *his* friend. I was the last remaining father figure.

Josie poured us a coffee – she appeared not to have heard about a beverage called tea – while Karl slipped from my grasp and slumped on a chair.

"You're both looking better," I said. And not just to bolster their confidence. If not exactly back to normal, they seemed to be recovering.

"The funeral went well," she said, stifling a sniff. "Almost too well. There were so many people they had to call in the police. Just to keep an eye on things. But there were no problems."

"Jonny was a much-loved man," I said. "Everyone I've spoken to has said so."

More sniffs: "I don't know how we'll cope without him."

Tears were not far away, so I kept on: "The DDR should be in good hands under Werner. He seems most capable."

"But he's not Jonny."

No arguing with that, so I merely said: "I'm sure Werner will carry on the good work. Meanwhile, I'm moving on. I've come to say goodbye."

At last, a hint of a smile: "With Frau Lindtner, I hear."

News travelled fast in Die Stadt. I said: "Trudi needed a break. But that doesn't alter what I said before: if you need help – are in any sort of trouble, you only have to pick up the phone. You have my number."

Remembering my recent conversation with Chief Inspector Fischer, I added: "You might also let me know if you hear anything about a man called Josef Feldmann."

"Ah yes, Sepp."

"You know him?"

"We've only met a few times, because he stays in Dresden and works on the boats, while I live here. But he and Werner are thick as thieves. Why do you ask?"

It did not seem a good idea to tell her Fischer had his eye on Feldmann as her husband's possible killer, so I took refuge in the obvious answer: that he had been the one to accuse me of the murder.

Josie nodded and said something about Feldmann always being around. A minor cog in the DDR machinery, but of little interest. I didn't pursue the matter.

As our conversation lapsed, a young voice piped up: "When are you going to take me to see Arsenal?"

It took me a second to mentally change gear from murder to football: "I'll check the fixture list when I get home; pick a good match."

"And you'll come here to see Hertha?" Karl was lively now, out of his chair.

"Of course. Told you I would." I had made rather a lot of footballing promises, but it would be months before Karl could cash in on them. I had the ungracious thought that he might forget the whole thing.

"Does that mean you'll be back here again?" asked Josie.

I hadn't given this any serious thought, but a promise is a promise, so I replied: "I suppose so. Not too sure when. The football season lasts until well into next year, so plenty of time."

"I'm not into football," said Josie, adding pointedly: "And Karl could do with some male company."

It wasn't until I was on my way back, after a flurry of farewell hugs and yet more promises, that the comment, 'Karl could do with male company', came back to me. Strange. Werner Breitling was a permanent fixture and certainly male; overwhelmingly male. That could only mean he was not 'company'. At least, not for young Karl. Something was rotten in the Kästner kingdom. And I was abandoning them. I felt a pang of guilt.

Eighteen

The following day Trudi and I fled. Packed a few belongings into my silver Porsche and headed east; actually, south to begin with, across the border into the Czech Republic, then a slow drift to wherever the fancy took us.

After several weeks, in early August, we found ourselves again in Saxony, but in an expat version in Romania. Very different from the Lindtner home on the Elbe.

Today almost every clan waves its own flag and wants a seat in the United Nations, but the nineteenth century was still the age of empire, Europe north of the Alps being under the control of just four powers: France, Germany, Russia and Austria-Hungary.

Trudi and I had been spending much of our time sauntering through the last of these, Hapsburg Greater Austria, where, in Victorian times, a bearded gaffer called Franz Josef ran an empire that comprised ten ethnic groups speaking fifteen different languages. With remarkably little friction. A mini United Nations under one master. Almost feudal.

When the call came, we happened to be in Sighisoara, one of a gaggle of Romanian 'Saxon' cities that are now almost entirely Romanian, their German ancestry confined to guide books, where they come under the heading of 'medieval pearls'.

By now I had discovered a personal pearl in Trudi, whom I'd better describe as 'mature' rather than 'medieval', if I'm to avoid summary chastisement. Human relations can be inexplicable. Maggie and I could hardly avoid clawing at each other. Now, for the first time in a quarter of a century I had a companion who was not intent on fighting. There had been a similar friction between Trudi and her daughter. Yet Trudi and I got on with barely a flurry to ruffle the waters. I can offer no reason for this; merely record that it was so.

Although our extended honeymoon remained blissful, I *was* starting to wonder where it would all end. Summer could not last forever. Neither could our tour. What then?

The call came, as I've said, in Sighisoara, and started as a text message. It was from Josie Kästner, who wanted to set up a time for a proper chat. I agreed one of her suggested slots, taking care to follow her final instruction: in future to *only ever* contact her on this, her new number. On no account was I to ring her old mobile. This could only mean one thing: she wanted to be away from the ears of Werner Breitling.

I agreed a time for early afternoon, when Werner would not be around. For privacy, Trudi and I returned to our hotel, one of our more atmospheric watering holes not far from Sighisoara's famous clocktower.

On the dot of 2pm, my phone sprang to life. It was Josie. We started with the usual 'catch-up' questions: how were we? Where were we? I kept my side of it concise, because this was *her* call; she was the important one. In reply to my return query, she replied:

"Okay." Without much conviction.

She would not have instigated proceedings had things been truly 'okay', so I said nothing. Waited for her to continue in her own time.

"It's August," she said at last.

I agreed that it was indeed the month of August.

"When everything shuts down," she continued. "People go off to the beach. Or the mountains. Even politicians give up being nasty to each other."

"So no excitement at the DDR?"

"Less to do, to be sure," she replied. "Which is why Werner wants me to take a holiday. Like everyone else."

Josie had rather evaded my question. Even in the silly season, the DDR might have something brewing. So I asked: "What about Werner? Will he also be going away?"

"Werner *never* stops. Even in August he'll find something to do."

"Such as?"

"I'm not sure. Which is why I was wondering if we might meet. For a longer chat."

"We're in *Romania*!" I exclaimed. Unnecessarily. I'd already told her that. "We're goodness knows how many hundreds of kilometres away from you."

"Werner says I should take at least two weeks off. Quite insistent. He wants me to see how they do things in Hungary, which must be something like halfway; maybe a couple of days' drive for each of us."

Two solid days behind the wheel! Just for a chat. The whole point of our trip had been sloth. No more than three hours on the road in any one day, four hours absolute maximum, then collapse into a suitable hostelry for several days of mooching around. But there was a sense of desperation in Josie's request. She didn't seem the sort who would drive for days purely on a whim. Or expect anyone else to do the same.

So I said: "Hang on. I'll consult madam."

I explained the situation to Trudi, who had already guessed the gist of it.

She didn't hesitate: "If Josie has problems, we go. Wherever it takes."

Returning to Josie, I said: "Madam agrees. Where do you want to meet?"

"My geography isn't too good… Never been much outside Germany… As I said, Werner's interested in Hungary. Can I leave you to find a place there?"

"Okay. Give us a few minutes. I'll ring back."

"*This* number, remember. Not the old one."

Josie *was* jumpy. I assured her I would get the right number, then rang off and explained the situation to Trudi, who fired up her smartphone.

"Google says the distance between us is 1,256 kilometres. The drive one way will take 13 hours 3 minutes."

"On the button," I said. "Because Google never lies."

Trudi smiled. "Josie's wheels may be slower than Google's."

I nodded. "Her Dacia did look a bit of a wreck."

"Your Porsche seems to think it's a Formula One; surprised you've not yet got a ticket. We should be a good deal faster."

I'd been looking at my Europe road atlas and reported: "Josie's part will be mostly on motorways, while we'll have to negotiate slower stuff in Eastern Europe. However, Josie's slower driving will be boosted by good roads, while my Formula One won't count for much in rural Romania. So our average speeds should be much the same."

Trudi said: "Throw in road works, accidents, comfort stops; we really haven't a clue how long it'll take."

"Only need a ballpark figure," I said. "So let's divide Google by two. The result is 600 kilometres and six-and-a-half hours. For each driver. Over two days that's less than four hours a day. Can't complain about that."

Trudi smiled. "I never complain. So where should we meet?"

"Obviously about halfway, but don't let's get too pedantic." I'd been studying the road map and continued: "Josie wants to see Hungary, which we went through on our way out. Remember that B&B in Visegrad?"

"The place with the Danube view and Rottweiler."

I nodded. "Attila the Rottweiler. To begin with you were scared of him. Big dog, bad name. But it wasn't long before you were slobbering over each other. Disgusting!"

"I didn't know Rottweilers were so sloppy."

"Don't bank on all of them being like that. But you and Attila certainly hit it off."

"Let's see, then…"

Trudi went back to her box of tricks. After a few moments, she reported back: "Sighisoara to Visegrad is 699.5 kilometres and 7 hours 57 minutes."

"I love the half-kilometre," I said. "Rounded up, that's 700 clicks and eight hours. Spread over two days. Easy. Okay by you?"

"Anything to see Attila again."

"I'll put this to Josie," I said. "Visegrad is closer to her than to us, so we would be doing her a favour."

I punched in her number, taking care to use the new one. She answered at the first ring.

I explained our thinking, which she accepted without comment; declared herself ready to set off the next day. I said I would try and book two rooms at our old B&B, one for Trudi and me, and one for her. When I realised there had been no mention of her son, I asked: "Will Karl be coming?"

"Karl's at summer camp. Near Braunlage in the Harz. He's been promised lots of old ladies on broomsticks, so was very excited. The Harz is witch country."

"He's not scared of witches?"

"Karl's not the scaredy sort. Sometimes I wish he'd be more careful."

"Boys will be boys. Good for him." Easy for me to say, because he was not my son.

We agreed to meet three days hence at 'Donaublick' in Visegrad. When we'd been there before I'd asked my hostess, a middle-aged lady with her hair tied back in a bun, why her house was called 'Danube view' in German. Was this not Hungary? Her reply had been that Visegrad was a small place that relied almost entirely on the holiday trade, much of it international. She had pointed out that not many people understood Hungarian – an understatement, as it's unlike anything else, impenetrable to foreigners. Her house had been 'Donaublick' since the days of the Hapsburgs, had kept going nicely under that name, and no one had got round to changing it.

The meeting with Josie having been settled, Trudi and I wandered out for a last look at Sighisoara. And later, our last meal in Romania. The next serious stop would be Visegrad. In the country of Attila the Hun and Attila the Rottweiler.

Nineteen

I didn't make a note of how close we came to Google's estimate of 7 hours 57 minutes. Roadworks were few, accidents zero, comfort stops plenty. We overnighted somewhere in eastern Hungary and pulled up outside Donaublick on the second day in early afternoon. Like 'sea views' the world over, to call it 'Danube View' was stretching a point: one almost needed to be in the attic with a telescope. But it was clean, comfortable, cheap and run by a motherly sort who couldn't do enough for her guests.

Frau Molnar, the lady in question, greeted us. I should really use the Hungarian for 'Mrs.', but don't know what that is. She was always 'Frau' to us, Hapsburg style, like her house. Visegrad is only a couple of hours by car from Austria, so German was her second language.

Our arrival was accompanied by barking off-stage. When Frau Molnar saw it was us, she released her hound, who came bounding out, full of the joys. I was granted a perfunctory sniff and deemed friendly. But uninteresting. For Attila, the smell that counted was Trudi's.

The dog sat down in front of her, a yellow tennis ball locked in his jaws. Expectant.

"Drop it", commanded Trudi, pointing at the ground.

Those words from me would have had no effect, but from Trudi…

Attila dropped the ball. Sat there looking up with big, pleading eyes. Trudi picked up the ball and threw it down the front garden.

Attila would have been happy to continue the game all day and into the following one, but humans soon tire of doggy sports, so after a couple of minutes we unloaded our bags and followed Frau Molnar into the house.

"Do you ever have guests that Attila does *not* like?" I asked.

She hesitated. "Not often."

"What then?"

I keep him shut up in the kitchen until they've gone."

I wondered what would happen if Attila then escaped. A Rottweiler in a bad mood is not an asset in the hospitality business. Soon to arrive would be Josie Kästner, who, if appearances were anything to go by, should harbour all sorts of interesting smells for the discerning hound. Would they be attractive smells?

Josie was taking her time, so much so that Frau Molnar was treating us to afternoon tea in the back garden when we heard the sound of a car drawing up and a couple of 'whoofs' from Attila.

I sprang to my feet, but Frau Molnar calmed me down. An expert on her pet, she knew these were exploratory 'whoofs', friendly, not aggressive.

She was right. By the time we arrived at the front of the house, all we could see of Attila was a disappearing rump and wagging tail, as he tore after a tennis ball. Standing beside a blue Dacia was Josie, a smile on her face.

It was several weeks since I had last seen her and told myself this *had* to be Josie. Because this was a girl who played hard to recognise. Her hair was no longer crimson but cobalt blue; down to the roots, so she was now looking after herself properly. The lower lip jewel had vanished. And she had given up those amateur dramatics skirts for a pair of fashionable ripped-to-shreds jeans. But the biggest change was physical. Her figure had gone from being slight to downright skinny.

This could hardly be healthy, but she seemed spritely enough; and cheerful. She apologised for being late and explained she had got lost in Vienna; gone round the city twice.

Hearing this, Trudi burst into song: "Wien, Wien, nur du allein, sollst stets die Stadt meiner Träume sein…" meaning 'Vienna, only you alone shall be the city of my dreams'. She tried to substitute 'dreams' for 'nightmare', but couldn't make it work, so we had a bit of a laugh. Everyone on good form. Except for Attila, who was sitting there, ball in mouth, waiting for the order, 'Drop it!' No one took a blind bit of notice. A dog's life.

Due to her motorway meanderings, Josie had missed out on lunch and announced she could do with some food. With her fragile build she would probably disappear down the nearest plughole without prompt refuelling, so even though Trudi and I had barely digested Frau Molnar's sticky cakes, I suggested we seek sustenance as soon as everyone was ready.

Visegrad is a small place, stretching in a narrow sliver for a couple of kilometres along the river. Donaublick was not that far from the centre, but as we were on holiday and devoted to sloth, I suggested we help wreck the planet and drive. I was voted the more reliable navigator, so we took the Porsche rather than the Dacia.

Although Visegrad exists for tourism, it does not take full advantage of its Danube-side location. The two main sights, the ruins of the royal palace and castle, lie a little way inland, as they have for centuries: little to be done there. Less understandable is that Highway Eleven from Budapest occupies pride of place along the Danube, relegating downtown Visegrad to a modest position away from the river. There is one exception, which was our target for tonight.

Hungarian is a language unlike any other, a meaningless jumble to foreigners, but one word had jumped out at me: 'Etterem'. It sounded like an 'eatery' and that's what it turned out to be: a restaurant. I was pointing our Porsche towards the 'Etterem' with the best view in town, just above the landing stage where Danube river traffic moored up.

The scene was not unlike Trudi and Josie's home town, the place where my European tour had first departed from its script, but the Danube here was rather wider than the Elbe. And now, towards the end of summer, the water level was lower. A more obvious difference was the river traffic: no old paddle steamers like the Kurort Rathen, but a sleek modern three-decker called 'Primus'. This was the 'Danube Bend', which featured in every Hungarian tourist blurb. Much to look at if the conversation flagged.

Not that the conversation *should* flag. We had driven hundreds of miles to hear what Josie had to say. At first she was reluctant to open up. To fill the gap, Trudi and I were full on for a good twenty minutes, Josie asking all the right questions, before I realised that a blow-by-blow account of our expedition was not what we were here for.

So when our monologue arrived at a suitable break, I asked: "What news of the German Democratic Right under its new leader?" I knew nothing beyond the fact that Werner Breitling had been duly elected.

A pensive smile from Josie. "Well… Werner is now in command. Doing his own thing."

"Which is?"

She shrugged. "Jonny and I always discussed DDR policies. Even when he moved to Dresden we'd have long chats, either over the phone or when he came to take Karl out. I wasn't just the drudge who kept the party machine going."

"But now you *are* that drudge?"

"Werner doesn't tell me much."

"You must have *some* inklings?"

"I still do all the paperwork: membership renewals, financial spreadsheets, getting posters printed. But for anything in the *future*… all he tells me is that we must be more 'proactive'."

"Meaning what?"

"To get people to listen to us we should do something exciting. Increased visibility would bring in more members."

"What's he getting at? Stunts?"

"I'm not sure… But he's very interested in Hungary. Says it's the country that's setting the example for the rest of us. So it was lucky for me that you happened to be staying in that direction."

"But Werner doesn't know you're seeing us, does he?"

"Good heavens, no! And it must stay that way. You must *only* contact me on my new number."

I didn't like the sound of this, so asked: "Is he threatening you?"

"No, no. It's just that Werner can be… rather protective. You met him once, remember?"

I nodded. "Not a pleasant experience."

"Some people do find him intimidating."

"Doesn't he mind you driving all this way on some wild goose chase?"

"Werner calls it gathering information. His idea of a holiday – even for other people – is a working one."

"I still don't understand what makes Hungary so special."

Josie looked at me as though I was stupid. "It's the way they deal with immigrants, of course."

"You mean that fence they've built?"

She nodded. "A wall, rather than just a fence. Very successful at keeping them out. Werner wants me to check on how they do it."

"Seems we can't get away from walls," I mused. "No sooner have we lost the Iron Curtain and Berlin Wall, than barriers start sprouting in other places. Israel to keep out the Palestinians; Americans to stop the Mexicans. Now also the Hungarians…"

"What would *you* do?" Josie's tone was quite aggressive. In spite of any differences she might have with Werner, they were both addicts of the far right.

With no easy answer, I just shrugged.

"We're being *invaded*," she insisted. "Can't just sit on our backsides and do nothing."

"There's precious little you and Werner can do," I pointed out. "Hungary is only getting away with it on her southern border because Serbia is outside the EU. We've just driven from Austria, through Hungary to Romania and back again. Free movement, because these countries are all in the European Union. Germany has no borders with non-EU countries, so there's no chance you could do anything like Hungary."

"Like a bet?"

"It would be illegal. You wouldn't get away with it."

"Wouldn't be illegal if the government decided to do it. The Austrians are already talking about putting a fence along the Brenner. That's the border with Italy, which *is* in the EU."

"The DDR isn't the government. And unlikely to be so." I hadn't meant to be so blunt, but Josie was becoming annoying.

"The old parties are dying. Public opinion is heading our way. Next thing we'll be a coalition with the AfD. Just you see."

Trudi had been mostly listening, but now joined in: "You said Werner wanted to be more proactive. Would that include trying to put a barrier on the Czech border?"

For some moments Josie did not reply, absentmindedly driving a piece of fish round her plate with a fork. Finally: "Anything could happen. And you haven't heard that from me."

"The police would never allow it," I said.

"Of course not. But it would be fantastic publicity."

"Would *you* support it?"

Josie shrugged. Would say no more. Left us with the implication she might not be too keen on Werner Breitling's proactive schemes.

The conversation drifted to other subjects, during which I asked if there was any prospect of finding Jonny's killer. Nothing new, apparently. She seemed disinterested, as though her husband's death and subsequent funeral were best forgotten. Time to look to the future. This was probably for the best, so I asked:

"What exactly *does* Werner want you to do in Hungary?"

"Inspect their fence. And talk to someone involved. He has a contact in a place called Mohacs. Like to come along?"

I glanced at Trudi, who hesitated, then nodded. We had no fixed plan, so why not.

Josie smiled. "Good to have company. Is tomorrow too early?"

I shook my head. "As long as Trudi can tear herself away from Attila.

Frau Lindtner squeezed my hand and smiled, so I announced:

"Okay. Dawn patrol it is. Target Mohacs.

Twenty

If two cars are headed for the same destination I'm not a fan of the convoy. It's all too easy for the vagaries of traffic to split you up. Better for both to be independent. However, Josie had managed to get lost in Vienna, so how would she cope with the equally challenging sprawl of Budapest?

In the end, we compromised. We would try the convoy system, but cater for a probable divorce by having Trudi travel as co-pilot with Josie in the Dacia, two pairs of eyes being better than one. After setting up their Satnav, I announced:

"It's another lovely day, ladies. So if all else fails, make use of the sun. Which usually rises in the east and sets in the west. Our route takes us almost due south, so unless you're on a short wriggle, the sun should start in front and to the left of you, then move across, still to your front, as the day wears on. If you find the sun *behind* you for any length of time, it means you'll soon be in Slovakia: if you're *really* dozy, you might even manage a dip in the Baltic."

Trudi was not amused, just informed me they'd be fine. Josie, hardly in a position to say anything, said nothing.

We set off according to plan A, which went well as far as Szentendre, but as we entered the Budapest suburbs my own navigation became the priority. I'll never know where they lost me. One moment they were snug in my rear view mirror, the next they were gone. Not to worry. I pressed on with plan B, as agreed. Once clear of the big city everything loosened up again and I arrived outside the Szent Janos Hotel in Mohacs just after 2.30.

I'd booked two rooms and managed to check into ours straight away, explaining that the others would follow in due course. When this would be was anyone's guess, so I set off for a look at the town, famous as a battlefield; actually, two battles, both several centuries ago. Ancient warfare was evidently the big thing in Mohacs, which sported several military statues, a large modern battlefield church, an armour-clad warrior and a tombstone dated 1526, which might even have been genuine. After a passing glance at the town hall, a jaunty confection of green domes, with yellow and pink façade, I returned to the Szent Janos, expecting to see a blue Dacia parked outside. It was not there.

I wasn't really concerned. They had my number and would have phoned if in any sort of trouble. It was probably just a case of girlie gossip making them forget the outside world.

By the time the Dacia finally showed up I was downing my first beer. They emerged giggling, apparently oblivious to the fact they had taken about twice as long as me.

"Lost again?" I asked, showing more irritation than intended.

"We took the scenic route – wherever that was," admitted Trudi. "Then a break for lunch. Hope you weren't worried."

"Well, you're here now," I said, simmering down. "Josie needs to check in, then it'll be time for a drink. And food."

"And meet Frank," added Josie.

"Who's Frank?"

"Werner's contact. Frank knows I'm coming and has said he'll meet me in the hotel at seven."

"Does he know you have company?"

Josie shrugged. "Does it matter?"

"I thought you didn't want Werner to know I was involved. When Frank reports back to Werner, he's bound to mention talking to us."

"I'll be the one reporting back. Not Frank."

"Even so… There may be leaks."

Josie pondered for a moment, as though it was something she had not considered. Then burst out:

"Sod it! I'm fed up with all this secrecy. What if Werner *does* get to know?"

This was quite a change. I wondered if she was being wise. Maybe distance was making her reckless. But it was her decision. I also wanted to know more about this barbed wire border, so Hungary's representative of the far right would be entertaining three of us.

Twenty-One

Hungary is high on any list of 'foodie' nations. Even in Communism times, when in most workers' paradise countries eating was little more than a mechanical function to keep body and soul together, it ran a decent cuisine. This pattern has not changed. Russia would still be amongst the first to be kicked out of any cooking contest, closely followed by the Czechs, but we'd had some excellent meals in Hungary. I was looking forward to seeing what sort of place our host would pick for us in Mohacs.

Ferenc – Frank to us – was small and slight, with fair hair and downy stubble on his chin. He had to be at least mid-twenties, but looked younger. At his age Russian would no longer have been a compulsory school subject, but he also had no German. He was of the pop culture, internet and social media generation, which operated in English, where he was idiomatic and fluent. As was Josie. Only Trudi was out of her linguistic comfort zone, but spending a few hours with English would be good practice for her.

Frank marched us out of the Szent Janos, saying he could offer us something better, which turned out to be a ten-minute walk away, just off the main square. It was a light and airy place, with metal chairs and tables, modern rather than traditional. Hungarian portions tend to be almost too generous, so I ordered just a húsleves, which came under 'Starters', but was a large bowl of chicken, dumplings and vegetable stew; a meal in itself. A beer to wash it down and we were ready for Josie to get to work on Frank.

"So how's your migrant situation?" she began. Immigration control was the main plank of all the far-right parties.

Frank allowed himself a smirk: "We don't have a migrant situation. Not any longer."

"Not at all?"

"Not at all. Mass population movements are like water; they take the paths of least resistance. If you build a dam – and our borders are now well dammed – any floods seek somewhere easier. Greece, Italy, Spain, France; we don't care a shit as long as this poison doesn't come near us."

I felt like telling Frank to mind his language, but wimpishly hesitated and heard Josie ask:

"Your fence is that effective?"

"A double barrier of razor wire, four metres high. How would *you* tackle that?"

"I wouldn't."

"Exactly. Anyone stupid enough to try would…" Frank gave a giggle. "Would risk having his family jewels ripped off."

He really used the expression 'family jewels'. Amazing what they teach in language school these days. He continued giggling to himself, as though the notion of migrants having their balls ripped to shreds was hugely entertaining. Trudi did not look amused. Even Josie, who must have shared his general outlook, seemed uncomfortable.

"Our land border is now pretty well invasion proof," he continued. "But here in Mohacs we have another problem: the Danube. Migrant infiltration by water."

"Yeah, I looked at a map," said Josie. "Like us on the Elbe, this is border country."

"Similar, but different. You only have one border to worry about." He held up one finger to underline the point. "Here it's more complicated. From Esztergom in the north all the way down here to Mohacs, the Danube flows within Hungary, but just downstream from us it hits a border triangle; becomes an international division, with Croatia on the west bank, Serbia on the east. So our customs and immigration post is pretty important. It can take hours for boats to pass through."

He sat back with a grin, as though making life difficult for river traffic was something to be proud of.

"That accounts for the legal stuff," he continued. "But imagine what it must be like for any darkies who chance their arm with a swim. The Danube is a damned sight colder than anything in Africa and they'll be going *against* the current. Battling through water as though your life depended on it – which it probably does – only to find yourself going backwards. Isn't that the funniest thing you ever heard?"

Frank collapsed in a paroxysm of mirth. He seemed unaware that his audience was not responding. Even Josie looked shocked.

"Is all this government approved?" I asked

"It's government *instigated*. The Fidesz party does not mess about. Unlike in Germany. And…" glancing at me "… in England."

"I'm here because the German Democratic Right intends to do something about it," said Josie. Her tone was uncertain, as though just starting to realise the implications of stemming Third World immigration.

"Good for you," said Frank. "Tomorrow we'll visit a section of the wall and take a trip on the river. Show you how it's done."

Cocky bastard!

But we just nodded and said nothing. My Hungarian cuisine appeared less tasty than before.

Twenty-Two

Frank delivered, as promised. We inspected miles of razor wire that could stop a tank, never mind some undernourished desperado from the Congo.

We took a short Danube cruise to visit the customs house, a modern three-storey structure that for some reason lay further from the border, upstream of Mohacs. Frank was clearly a frequent and welcome visitor, much joking with the lads and lasses. A cruiser of the sort that carries about 200 passengers was moored below, undergoing clearance. Pointing at it, Frank said:

"They're having fun with that one. Most of the boats are old hands at the game and know all the tricks, but she's a Danube virgin: can't hope to get all her paperwork in order first time out. They'll be stuck here for hours."

Another bout of giggles, as though constructing a mountain of red tape was a comedy show. It wasn't only immigrants who were being done over on the border.

By the end of the day, even Josie had had enough. When Frank suggested another dinner out, the three of us claimed extreme fatigue; an early night and all that. We were certainly tired, but our overriding aim was to get rid of Frank. We parted with lashings of bonhomie, promises to keep in touch, the best hypocrisy we could muster.

As Frank disappeared out of the Szent Janos front door, I gasped: "I need a drink!"

The girls followed and we ordered something strong. When we had settled, I commented (back now in German): "An interesting day."

I kept my opening remark deliberately neutral. Waited to see what the others would say.

Trudi was the first to show her colours: "What a horrid young man!"

That's what I loved about Trudi. Wore her heart on her sleeve.

I nodded. "Rather over the top."

Josie said: "But useful info on how we might control migrants." She sounded thoughtful rather than enthusiastic, as though Frank's insensitive performance had left its mark.

"We've seen what Mohacs has to offer, so what now?" I asked. Trudi and I would doubtless continue our European wanderings, having only diverted to southern Hungary to keep Josie company, so the question was really directed at her.

After a moment's thought, she replied: "Head for home, I suppose. Which will take a few days. When I get back I'll tell Werner what we've seen."

"I thought Werner wanted you gone for a couple of weeks," I said.

"He said I should take two weeks off. Away from the office; away from work. But once I've checked out Hungary, it's up to me. A lot needs doing at home; stuff that Jonny used to see to.

And in a week Karl's summer camp ends. I'll have to be back by then."

"Reckon you can manage to get home on your own?" I asked. So far she had not shown much navigational expertise.

"Of course I can manage!" Josie was quite offended. "Return the way I came. Easy."

"Things look different when you're facing the other way."

"No problem," she insisted. "Tomorrow I'll drive back to Donaublick; say hello to Attila, spend the night. Then home in two days. I'm not a baby."

The question was not whether Josie was a baby, but if she could cope with Europe's roads. I had no desire to nursemaid her all the way back to Germany, so kept any misgivings to myself.

After that, we did indeed have an early night. Frank had been hard work, our claim to fatigue genuine. In spite of that, neither Trudi nor I found it easy to sleep; too many impressions swirling around in our brains.

"I'm worried about Josie," she said. "Remember, I spent a whole day with her on the way down."

"Plenty of girlie chat?"

"I'd never really talked to her before. Although living in the same town, until yesterday I knew next to nothing about her. But once she got going, I couldn't stop her."

"Complete life story?"

"More or less. Starting with the usual teenage crush. A handsome young devil called Jonny Kästner. To earn his approval, she bought into his theology of political extremism: Germany for Germans, out with foreigners; especially those that looked different. Then she got pregnant, not entirely planned, I gathered. Leaving her stuck with *two* of Jonny's children: the DDR and Karl."

"Until Jonny was killed," I said.

"Not merely killed, but murdered. A double trauma."

"Did she have any idea who might have done it?"

"More than an idea. She was pretty sure. Said it had to be Sepp Feldmann."

"The Kurort Rathen crewman. Also Chief Inspector Fischer's main suspect. Only there's not enough evidence to hold him."

"Josie said to begin with she was too shattered to think straight. But gradually, after the funeral, when she saw Werner and Sepp together in secretive huddles, things began to fall into place. She says Feldmann is Breitling's Rottweiler."

"A slur on Attila."

"Not every Rottweiler is like a softie like Attila. They have a reputation."

"But Werner and Josie are lovers," I objected.

"Were. Past tense. When Jonny moved out to be nearer his troops, Josie still felt the need for a man about the house. Breitling was probably the only candidate. But as her mind cleared and he became chief suspect, she indicated he was no longer welcome."

Do you think Breitling realises why he's been booted out?"

"Must do."

"Which means Josie could be in danger."

Trudi considered this for a moment; gave a wriggle beside me to find a more comfortable position and said:

"Surely not… Breitling might get away with one murder, but *two*…? He must realise the police will be watching him."

"We already know Breitling can't have been the one to wield the knife, because he has a cast-iron alibi," I replied. "We're assuming Feldmann did the deed on Werner's behalf. What if the DDR's new leader reckons the remaining Kästner is becoming too dangerous and must also be eliminated? And orders Beer-Gut Feldmann to strike again. The beauty of this from his point of view is that if anything goes wrong and the situation becomes too hot, it should be easy to cast Feldmann adrift. I can just see Werner, all wide-eyed innocence, saying to Fischer: 'Nuffink to do wiv me, guv. If Sepp says otherwise, he's just trying to offload some blame. Between ourselves, we'd been having a bit of falling out…' And so on, in a similar vein.

"I don't think it'll come to that." Trudi sounded as though she was trying to convince herself rather than me.

"Well, there's not much we can do about it," I said. "Except perhaps warn Josie. Who must realise anyway she might be in the firing line."

We churned the problem back and forth a while longer, without coming to any firm conclusion. Eventually, I slipped into a disturbed sleep.

Twenty-Three

Next day we parted company. Josie headed for home, still saying she would retrace her route out, as this was familiar territory. She had taken quite a shine to Attila, so might spend a couple of nights at Frau Molnar's. Still being on holiday, there was no hurry, but eventually she would report back to Werner on Hungary's migrant defences. Then fetch Karl from his summer camp in the Harz.

Although feeling a twinge of guilt at allowing Josie to return on her own, I told myself she was a grown woman, perfectly capable of looking after herself. Even if she drove round Vienna half a dozen times, she should eventually find the right road back. And once home, Werner couldn't possibly attempt anything lethal with the police watching his every move. Could he?

I tried to dismiss Josie from my mind and instead concentrated on planning what *we* might do next. Truth to tell, the idea of spending a carefree summer exploring Europe was starting to wear thin. A gap year might *sound* wonderful, but I had always led an active life and was beginning to think that just a gap *summer* was probably enough. Trudi was in a similar situation, having taken a deserved break from the slog of running a hotel, but could now do with something to get her teeth into again. Neither of us was ready for a life of unremitting sloth, yet neither of us had anything to go back to.

It was in this uncertain frame of mind that Trudi suggested we try a beach or two. So far we had been culture vultures; maybe it was time for a change. The idea had first been mooted in landlocked Hungary, during one of our chats with Frau Molnar, who enjoyed the social interaction with her customers as much as the cash it brought in.

She had pointed out that although Hungary's beaches were now restricted to the crowded shores of Lake Balaton, it had not always been so. When the World War One peace treaties had stripped Hungary of much of its territory, its leader, Admiral Horthy, had become an 'Admiral' with no coastline – his only fleet a few toy boats amongst the bathing beauties of Balaton. But as a young man, Horthy had joined a proper navy, the proud arm of the Austrian Empire, with bases in the Adriatic. Anyone in Hapsburg-lands fancying some sun and sand only had to hop on a train to Trieste, from where there were plenty of home-grown Riviera spots to choose from.

Frau Molnar had been an excellent sales rep for the glories of this Hapsburg past, so Trudi and I decided to test her advice. During the past century there had been some changes – our transport no longer a train, but my silver Porsche. And we now had frontiers to contend with. Austria and Hungary had become landlocked; Trieste was in Italy; Slovenia had been granted a tiny coastal strip to include the old Venetian port of Piran; while in the south it was Croatia most of the way to Montenegro.

Frau Molnar's top tip had been Opatija, now in Croatia. As this was also on the closest stretch of coast after a tedious two-day drive from Mohacs, it seemed a suitable spot for our initial slump.

Trudi and I sauntered around the lush vegetation of the botanic garden pretending to be royalty; emperors Franz Josef of Austria and German Kaiser Wilhelm had met here. We swam off the ornate Hotel Kvarner and took the little yellow glass-bottomed water taxi.

One day was spent in nearby Rijeka, a city with a confusing history: during the Twenties it had been the personal fiefdom of an adventurer called d'Annuncio, after which it went to Italy as Fiume, meaning 'river'; after World War Two it became part of Yugoslavia, retaining the same name, but now in Serbo-Croat.

After Opatija we had planned to move west into the Istrian Peninsula, to the Roman arena in Pula, the warm waters of the Adriatic and a galaxy of ancient Venetian towns.

We were enjoying a waterside fish dinner, washed down with an excellent Soave Classico, when my mobile rang. Few people had my number. Even fewer might need to contact me. Not my ex-wife, Maggie; that was for sure. Could it be Chief Inspector Fischer, with news about the Kästner murder? Or Josie? I could think of no one else.

The voice at the other end spoke accented German, which for a moment I couldn't place, until she said it was Frau Molnar.

I couldn't recall giving her my number, then realised this is often part of hotel check-in information.

"Yes…?"

"I'm sorry, but I don't know who else to ring. Have to tell someone. You see, Josie Kästner's vanished."

Panic competed with guilt as I asked: "What do you mean 'vanished'?"

"She… she's… gone."

"She was on her way home. Wasn't planning to stay."

"I know. But her car is still here. And she's taken Attila."

"Your dog has also disappeared?"

A snuffle at the other end. "I don't know what to do. *Both* of them. Vanished. Without a word."

I almost said 'and without a bark', but realised she might not find this amusing, so merely asked:

"Have you told the police?"

"Of course I have. They were polite but useless. Said people left all the time without giving a reason. Especially in the hotel trade."

"They're probably right. Josie said she was going and she has. She's not a very confident driver, so maybe she went home by train."

"But why leave her car in my drive? Without telling me. And why steal Attila? I know they'd become good friends, but he's *mine*."

"It's just a coincidence that Attila has gone. No connection."

"*Of course* there's a connection. Attila would never leave unless someone took him. If he'd been dog-napped, he'd have woken the whole neighbourhood and I'd have heard. He's very choosy. Doesn't take to everyone, and certainly not to a complete stranger. He *must* have gone with Josie."

I couldn't fault Frau Molnar's logic. Why Josie should abscond with her Rottweiler was beyond me, but I couldn't help being concerned. Not for one moment did I believe my own story that Josie had taken a train because she was too scared to drive. She may have been a poor navigator, but had seemed quite unruffled by the fact. Getting lost on the way down had not bothered her.

"What do you expect me to do?" I asked.

More snuffling: "She's *your* friend. I was hoping you could come back here and remove her car. It's taking up the space for my other guests."

"Difficult to move cars unless you have the keys."

"On TV everyone starts cars by fiddling with wires. Takes only a few seconds."

"That's on the telly," I replied. "I'm not a criminal or cop, who may know about such things.

"Well, I thought you might know something about that friend of hers."

That brought me up sharp.

"Friend?" I snapped. "What friend?"

"Maybe not exactly a friend, but she certainly knew him. He knocked on the door the second night she was here. Attila was locked up in the kitchen, which was lucky, because he set up an awful racket. He either likes or loathes someone's smell. Didn't like Josie's friend at all."

"What did this visitor look like?"

"Nothing special. German. Rather too well fed."

I must have shown some reaction, because Trudi touched my arm, asked if I was okay. I was very far from okay, as I put another question to Frau Molnar:

"You say this man knocked on the door and asked to see Josie. What happened next? Did he stay long? Did she go with him?"

"I didn't like to eavesdrop, so can't tell you what they talked about. But he didn't stay long. Five minutes max. I'm sure about that, because as soon as this bad smell had gone, Attila went quiet again. Josie tried to make light of it, said it was nothing important. And she'd be leaving next day as planned. That's the last I saw of her. And Attila. Must have left together, sometime during the night."

"I'm glad you called," I said. "We'll be back soon as we can. Give us a couple of days, as we're down in Croatia. But I'll try and find out what happened."

I rang off.

Trudi gave me a frightened look. "What's going on?"

I shrugged. "Not sure. But it sounds horribly like Beer-Gut Feldmann has been paying Josie a visit."

Trudi put a hand over her mouth. Whispered: "What do we do?"

"We finish our meal. Then a good night's sleep. After that... Well, we can forget Venetian towns, swimming in warm waters and Roman ruins. We'll have to return to Frau Molnar."

"By the time we get there it'll be far too late to do anything," said Trudi. "This must have happened days ago."

I nodded. "It may seem pointless. Probably *will be* pointless. But we can't just carry on as though nothing has happened. We owe it to Josie to do *something* ."

"You have Josie's phone number, why not try that first? See if she answers."

Trudi was right. Frau Molnar's call had upset me. I wasn't thinking straight; still blaming myself for letting Josie go back on her own. So I rang her number. No reply; just a request to leave a message. Which I did.

The phone in my hand reminded me of another possibility: Chief Inspector Fischer. If he could confirm that Josef Feldmann had never left Dresden that would eliminate one possibility.

It was getting late, but they say the law never sleeps, so I gave it a try. Tapped in Fischer's number. At this hour I only expected to find a minion who would ask me to leave a message, but to my surprise it was Fischer himself who took the call. He seemed confused when I gave my name, but it *had* been a while. And the media had been full of events in Chemnitz, another ex-Stasiland city, where right-wing protests had recently erupted into violence; fire bombs and police in riot gear. Stuff that would go straight to Fischer's desk at the BKA.

Then I realised there might be another reason for him being slow on the uptake. Apart from that brief episode with Frank in Mohacs, I had spent the past few weeks speaking nothing but German, which I was continuing to do now. But Fischer associated me with English. When I repeated my greeting in that language he immediately made the connection.

"Ah yes, Mr. Blake. The Jonny Kästner case. Of course I remember. Nothing new to report, I'm afraid…"

His pause allowed me to get a word in: quite a few words. I brought him up to date on Josie's trip to meet us, our Hungarian border inspection and the phone call from Frau Molnar. I ended up by asking whether he knew the whereabouts of Josef Feldmann.

"Not offhand. Our resources are limited and we've had to concentrate on more recent events. The Kästner investigation has slipped a little. But I'll see what I can find out."

"Could you please email me a photo of Feldmann? Frau Molnar sounded pretty upset, so we'll have to drive back to Visegrad; see if there's anything we can do to help. If I can show her a picture of Feldmann, we should be able to establish whether he was Josie's visitor."

"Will do," Fischer replied. "And I'll let you know if anything else turns up."

We finished our meal in subdued mood. The evening that had started on a high was ending in foreboding.

As I waited to pay the bill, I said: "I still can't get my head round the timetable."

"What do you mean?"

"Both cars left Mohacs at the same time, right?

Trudi nodded.

"Even Josie couldn't have taken more than one day to get back to Frau Molnar's at Visegrad."

Again Trudi nodded at my silent query.

"She planned to stay two nights, so the disappearing act must have occurred on day three after leaving Mohacs."

"I think I see…" Trudi was beginning to grasp what I was driving at. "Meanwhile, we took two days to reach the coast and have been here for four nights…

"It's been six days since we left Mohacs, which means Josie must have vanished three days ago. Yet only now does Frau Molnar get round to ringing us."

"She wouldn't want to worry us at once. Probably expected Josie to turn up again."

"Three days is a long time to expect a guest with her car sitting in the drive to reappear."

"She said she tried the police."

"Hmm." I was not convinced. "Reminds me of the Sherlock Holmes story. *Hound of the Baskervilles*, I think. The mystery of the dog that did *not* bark in the night."

"Are you feeling okay?" Trudi was looking at me, quite concerned.

"Attila the Rottweiler, Hound of Visegrad, presents us with *two* mysteries: one, why did he bark like hell when Josie's visitor appeared at the door? And two, why did Frau Molnar not hear a sound as he vanished during the night?"

The waiter appeared with the bill; I paid.

Trudi took my hand. "What you need is some TLC."

I allowed myself to be led bedwards, but my performance was not up to my usual Casanova standard.

Twenty-Four

When we woke next morning, Josef Feldmann's image was already lodged in my phone. It was a head and shoulders shot, probably taken when he had been interviewed after Jonny's death. The prominent jowls and balding oval cranium made his head look bottom heavy; a well-fed face but not a healthy one. There was also a text message:

Last confirmed sighting of Feldmann in Dresden was seven days ago . Have passed relevant info to my opposite number in Budapest, but don't expect too much . Would appreciate an update after your meeting with Molnar. Take care.

That the Chief Inspector should sign off with 'Take care' was ominous. It now had to be a possibility that the man thought to have killed Kästner had left Germany and was indeed the person seen talking to his widow.

Google informed me that the road distance back to Visegrad was 558.3 kilometres and would take six hours and six minutes. Remembering our recent inspection of the Hungarian border and the fact it was still the holiday season, this timing seemed optimistic, so I decided to allow two days. With three days already gone since Josie's disappearance, a few hours more or less should make little difference.

My caution was justified when the Hungarian border turned out to be even worse than anticipated, a queuing time of nearly one hour before we got to present our credentials. Human paperwork was bad enough, but then they started on my Porsche: registration papers, MOT, insurance, etc. This was followed by a brusque: "open up". No 'please' or 'sir'. I opened the boot, thinking they might be looking for stowaways, but they seemed more interested in whether I had a warning triangle, spare bulbs, all the nonsense that bureaucracy now inflicts on foreign motorists. My accuser was starting on the lack of any hi-vis jacket when the fellow in the car behind me lost his cool. He was Hungarian and I guessed he was telling the official that his behaviour was guaranteed to wreck their country's tourist industry. At all events, it did the trick. With bad grace, I was permitted to enter the country.

As we drove on towards Lake Balaton, I reflected that Europe had once been littered with border crossings that could turn into nightmares if an official had got out of bed on the wrong side; we had become spoilt, accustomed to sailing unhindered across lines that now existed only on maps. Over much of the continent we could also pay in a common currency. The dream of a United Europe, realised in part by the Romans and attempted by Charlemagne, had finally come to pass.

But reality was starting to spoil the party. The super-state was being given the thumbs down as people returned to their historic tribes. Instead of coalescing, Europe was splintering, the Soviet Union and Yugoslavia already dead and buried. Although the EU was trying to fill the vacuum left by the broken Communist empires, recent experiences suggested that this system was also headed for the rocks. The European Union 'project' might have succeeded with just the founder members, France, Germany, Italy and the Benelux, but democracy had never been woven into the original DNA and the EU had now become too large and bureaucratic.

Worse still, a vital cog in this 'project', a common currency, had never been accepted by Britain or Scandinavia and was proving a disaster for the Mediterranean economies.

Above all, there was the spectre of uncontrolled immigration. Communities which, since the dawn of time, had been largely homogeneous, now found they were strangers in their own land. Most had wanted to do the decent thing – offer shelter and opportunity to those less well off, but it had been too much, too fast. And it was open-ended. The numbers from the Third World knocking on the door were virtually limitless.

Immigration. The reason I'd been given a hard time by that Hungarian border guard. The reason Jonny Kästner had founded the German Democratic Right. The reason we were on our way to try and solve the riddle of his vanished widow.

My thoughts were interrupted by Trudi:

"If Josie has disappeared, someone will have to fetch Karl."

I came to with a start. She was right. Back to practicalities. With everything else that had happened, I'd clean forgotten her son.

"When is summer camp supposed to end?" I asked.

"Can't remember. Must be around now."

"Do we know where summer camp is?"

"Somewhere in the Harz."

"A big area. With thousands of happy campers."

"Josie didn't seem to have many friends…" began Trudi, already speaking of her in the past tense.

I finished her thought: "So fetching Karl may be up to me. I seem to spend my time rescuing the poor lad."

"Let's hope all will be revealed when we reach Frau Molnar's," said Trudi, with a confidence she could hardly feel. Just trying to cheer me up.

I nodded; not because I agreed, but because there was nothing constructive I could say or do. Frau Molnar had sent out a cry for help and I'd felt obliged to rush to her rescue. With little prospect of being able to do anything.

My involvement in German far-right politics had come about through nothing more sinister than kicking a football on the banks of the Elbe. I knew nothing and cared even less... No, that was not true. I *did* care about Josie Kästner, little girl lost, now paying a heavy price for a teenage crush. I didn't like bullies and Werner Breitling was certainly a bully. As for Sepp Feldmann, he and I had history, but I was a mature man, able to take care of myself. The possibility that he might have Josie in his sights made me angry. Poor little painted Josie, who I was coming to look on almost as a wayward daughter.

There might not be much we could do when we reached Visegrad, but I would have a damned good try at finding out what was going on.

Twenty-Five

We drew up outside Donaublick in early afternoon on the following day, parking in the road, because Josie's blue Dacia was occupying what should have been our slot. Frau Molnar was a meticulous lady, who had converted her large Victorian house into three en-suite B&Bs, with corresponding spaces for their vehicles. Business was obviously good, her apartments all taken and her Skoda in the owner's position. Although two of the other spaces were currently empty, they were booked for guests due to arrive later. I could understand why she wanted to get rid of a useless car cluttering up her drive.

Trudi and I got out and stretched out legs. Budapest does not have a motorway ring and it had been a tedious crawl through its western suburbs. But the earlier rain had blown away, the sun was doing its best and we were ready to do business.

I rang the bell. This time there was no welcoming bark. On previous visits I had wondered at the wisdom of running an establishment like Donaublick with a Rottweiler on the premises, but Attila had always been well behaved and friendly. At least, with us. Now we could hear no canine welcome.

The door was quickly opened by the familiar figure of Frau Molnar, sixty-ish, homely, her greying hair tied back in a bun.

We each got a hug: "Can't thank you enough for coming back. Kettle's on the boil. I'll tell you what happened over a cup of tea."

"Nothing new to report?" I asked. "No Attila? No Josie?"

Frau Molnar shook her head. "It was so unexpected. Frau Kästner had settled her bill the night before, but should have been down for breakfast; after all, she'd paid for it. I have my own apartment at the back, away from the guests, but there's a small cooking area where I do the breakfasts and this is where Attila sleeps…"

"He didn't sleep with you? Say, on your bed?"

Frau Molnar gave a little shudder. "Certainly not! *So* unhygienic."

"But there was no sign of him?"

"I just stood there, staring at his empty bed. It was as though the sun had failed to rise at the proper time. His lead, which I was always careful to stow on a top shelf, had also gone. Then my first guests appeared. I asked if they'd seen Attila. They were equally puzzled. Said they'd heard no noises during the night. Nothing. The only thing I could think of was that Frau Kästner might have taken him into *her* room. Strictly forbidden of course, but they'd become *such* good friends and she might have wanted some protection…"

"Protection from her visitor?"

"She'd tried to dismiss him as unimportant, but he'd obviously left her shaken."

The tea had been poured and we were sitting down. I took out my phone and brought up the photo of Josef Feldmann.

"Was this the man?"

Frau Molnar nodded. Without hesitation.

"You're sure?"

"When you open a door to someone, it's face to face. Close. No mistake, it's him all right. Who is he?"

We're pretty sure he's the man who murdered Josie's husband."

"Then why's he still on the loose?"

Not enough evidence to arrest him."

"That's terrible… But that means…?"

I nodded. "Why we're concerned about Josie. You say she never turned up for breakfast. When did you find out she'd gone?"

"Almost at once. I was beside myself. Attila couldn't have simply vanished. So I knocked on Frau Kästner's door. No reply. It was unlocked, so I went in. The room was empty. Bed made up, looked as though it had never been slept in; keys on the bedside table; all personal effects gone."

"And no Attila."

Frau Molnar seemed close to tears. "No Attila. And Frau Kästner was such a nice girl… "

"We can at least take a look at her car," I suggested, more to give us something to do than in the hope of finding anything. It was a hatchback, everything inside visible, so could hide no nasty surprises: like a body.

"It's locked. And I haven't wanted to break in. But as you are her friends…"

I could take a hint as well as the next man: was being set up for some breaking and entering. Why not? We finished our tea, then trooped out to where the little blue Dacia was parked. It looked a mode of transport rather than anyone's pride and joy, with front end parking scratches half hidden by mud and that wing mirror still adrift, months after I'd first noticed it.

We tried the doors. Locked. Looked inside, which, surprisingly, was less scruffy, just a few supermarket bags in the back and one slim blue volume on the front passenger seat.

I made a round of inspection. All the windows were shut tight, so no way in there. Very well, let's try the obvious. I stood by the front offside wheel and indulged in some groping.

Bingo!

I withdrew my hand, which now contained a key.

I was rewarded with gasps of amazement. No member of the magic circle ever had a better audience.

Trudi: "That's amazing! How did you know…?"

I replied: "Oldest trick in the world. Especially popular with ladies, who often have pocket-less clothing and are forever losing their handbags: stick a spare key under a front wheel arch."

Trudi pointed out: "If everyone knows about that, the car could easily have been stolen."

"Of course. But who'd want to steal this wreck? More likely *arrange* to have it pinched and claim on the insurance."

I opened the door. Picked up the slim blue volume, which turned out to be a diary; looked in the glove compartment, which only contained the service manual and some music discs. There appeared to be nothing of interest in the car, except that diary, which I riffled through, revealing a mass of entries, both before and after our present date. I would study it later.

Josie Kästner had disappeared off the face of the earth, leaving no clues except her abandoned car. Kidnapped by Josef Feldmann? Maybe killed? With his background as Breitling's henchman and our suspicions about Jonny's death, that seemed all too likely. But how was such a scenario compatible with the simultaneous disappearance of Frau Molnar's Rottweiler?

And now the diary. No item is more personal. If I lost mine, with all that forward planning and secure information gone, I'd contemplate suicide. Yet Josie had left hers, lying like a flashing beacon on a front seat, having first 'secreted' the car key in the most obvious possible place. This was a diary begging to be found.

Finally there was the manner of her departure: bill paid, room tidy; no rushed job, well planned. It was as though she had *chosen* to go off alone with Feldmann, a man she had good reason to fear. Nothing made any sense.

Still, we had the diary. I held it up and said: "Josie's Rosetta Stone."

"Trudi: "*What* stone?"

I replied: "Ancient Egyptian script – hieroglyphics – had always been a mystery. No one could decipher it. Until one of Napoleon's soldiers found a stone with *three* different versions of the same event, including one in hieroglyphics and one in Greek. As Greek was a well-known language, scholars could work out what the hieroglyphics meant."

"Sounds complicated."

"Took years. *We* need to unlock the mystery of Josie's Rosetta Stone…" I waved the thin blue volume… "rather more quickly."

Frau Molnar, with her own priorities, said: "Just as long as her car is out of my drive tomorrow."

"It will be," I promised. "But first we have work to do. Come on, Trudi."

Twenty-Six

For dinner Trudi and I went back to our favourite Visegrad 'Etterem', perched on the banks of the Danube. After earlier rain, the evening had turned fine, if chilly: summer was drawing to a close, autumn in the air. This evening there was no steamer moored, no river traffic at all, just a bucolic scene of fields and woods on the opposite bank; still Hungary here, but due to become Slovakia a few miles upstream.

We were later than usual, having been immersed in Josie's diary. It was not that we were having difficulty working out what her personal hieroglyphics meant, even though these were often obscure and we had made little progress. No, we had been diverted by an entry that was perfectly clear and dated yesterday: 'summer camp ends': followed by a number.

If Karl's holiday in the Harz mountains was now officially over, his hosts would be wanting to get rid of him. Maybe that's where Josie had gone; if so, why had she abandoned her car without telling Frau Molnar? Maybe she had gone in Feldmann's car? No, that was ridiculous! Or was it? She had said she thought Feldmann was probably Jonny's killer, but what if that was just a smokescreen? What if she and Feldmann were in cahoots and it was Josie herself, not Breitling, who wanted Jonny Kästner dead? Had I not told myself before that many murders were family affairs?

I couldn't imagine the Josie I'd got to know as a killer, but I could be wrong. It *would* explain her disappearance. I was thoroughly confused.

However, there was one puzzle we should be able to sort out quickly. Against the 'summer camp ends' entry in her diary was a number, obviously a mobile. Why not give it a try?

I did and it was answered after the third ring. When I gave my name, the lady at the other end said she was glad I'd called because Karl should have been collected yesterday.

"So his mother has not been?" I asked. Maybe a silly question after that opening remark, but I needed to be sure.

"Of course not. Frau Kästner said she would not be able to manage. Told me someone else would be collecting the boy. Gave me your name. Didn't say you would be late."

The witch at the other end – the Harz was famous for its witches and she sounded like one – was obviously not pleased. I dreaded telling her I was phoning from Hungary and would need at least two days to get there, but there was no easy way out. I braced myself, asked for her address and said I would be along shortly."

"What do you mean by 'shortly'?" asked the witch.

"Maybe a couple of days," I replied. And rang off before I could hear her reply.

"This gets weirder by the moment," I said.

"Karl's been expecting you?" asked Trudi, who had been following the gist from my side of the conversation.

I nodded. "Josie obviously told them Karl might be picked up by someone else. And mentioned me. How could she possibly know Frau Molnar would phone us and we would come running?"

"Maybe Frau Molnar is also in on it."

Frau Molnar as a participant, not a helpless bystander, was not something I'd considered. It seemed unlikely, but we were mired in a miasma of unlikeliness. *One* of these seemingly impossible options *had to* be the answer.

"I no longer know what to believe," I said. "But we can think about that later. Right now my priority has to be fetching Karl."

"What will you do with him? Where will you take him?"

"Home." As I said it, I realised Karl no longer had a home. At least, nowhere he would be looked after. He was effectively an orphan. In the short term, his only obvious guardian was a middle-aged Englishman, who had foolishly agreed to kick a football about with him. The mess I was now in was almost worse than living with my ex, Maggie.

"Until we can get something sorted, he'll have to stay with us at the hotel," said Trudi.

She sounded less than enthusiastic, but what could we do? Social services, or some such, would eventually take little Karl Kästner off our hands, but until then he was ours.

"Seems we have little choice," I said. "If you're happy to drive Josie's car back…"

Trudi nodded. Without looking particularly happy.

"*I'll* be off to the Land of Witches to fetch Karl. Meet you back in the hotel. In about three days from now."

"Might be an idea to bring that police friend of yours up to date," said Trudi.

"Ah, yes. Chief Inspector Fischer. Will do. And I'll start trying to decipher the diary."

"Don't forget Attila."

"What about him?"

"A disappearing Rottweiler must be part of the jigsaw."

"Must he!"

Trudi was right, but I was becoming overwhelmed by the sheer weight of conflicting evidence. I wanted to shut down. Disappear to a desert island. Anything.

"Come on. Beddy-byes." The bill had been paid and Trudi took my hand.

I allowed myself to be led away.

Later, my Casanova rating took a further knock. And I slept badly.

Twenty-Seven

According to Google, the distance from Visegrad to Karl's summer camp at Braunlage was 940 kilometres and would take 10 hours 14 minutes. Too far for one day, especially as I needed some time on the phone with Fischer. Although in a slower car, Trudi should be able to get home the same day.

Fond farewells over, Trudi squeezed into Josie's Dacia, while I took the helm of my Formula One. Now firmly back in the European Union, where free movement was part of their religious creed, we should have no further border problems, just the usual imponderables of variable infrastructure and roadworks.

I first called Chief Inspector Fischer after breakfast, but he had been busy; try again later. A few miles the other side of Bratislava I found a coffee and comfort stop and did as asked.

Second time lucky. He could afford a few minutes. After I had established that there was no further news of either Josie or Feldmann, I gave a rather chaotic account of what I'd been doing; chaotic because all my theories about the situation were clearly nonsense.

When I'd finished, Fischer said: "I'm glad you called, because our focus is returning to the German Democratic Right party. The Chemnitz riots have kept us busy for a while, but they're now contained and we're seeing increased levels of activity from Breitling's lot.

"What sort of activity?"

"Emails… phone calls. Nothing you can put your finger on, because they know we're watching and listening; being very careful. But something seems to be in the offing. You say you have Frau Kästner's diary; we'd like to have a look at it."

"You know what diaries are like: scrawls known only to the author."

"Wouldn't need the whole year. But the next few weeks would be helpful. Could you let me have photos of those pages?"

"I'm on the road at the moment, so can't manage anything until tonight."

Fischer had to accept that, but I didn't want to let him go quite yet, so I asked:

"It's getting on for a week since Josie Kästner and Feldmann vanished. What theories do you have?"

"Difficult to say. We're keeping an eye on things."

"Come on! Give me a break… Helmut."

I remembered our first meeting, all those weeks ago, when we had dined on the banks of the Elbe. The Chief Inspector had been in expansive mood, saying he liked to mix business with pleasure. It had been a casual affair, pleasure predominating, so he had offered an evening of first names: Ed and Helmut.

Now, over the phone, I had jogged his memory with another 'Helmut'.

There was a chuckle from the other end. Then: "Very well… Ed. This is our current thinking: the DDR was founded by Jonny Kästner and his young – very young – girlfriend, Josie. Not headline news, because in Germany political parties come and go like April showers – usually they're just as brief. However, the DDR has managed to keep its head above water; made steady if unspectacular progress, mainly in Saxony, Brandenburg and Mecklenburg-Vorpommern; our eastern states. Then, as immigration became the key issue, right-wing parties started to flourish. The main contender was Alternative for Germany, but hanging onto its coat-tails, offering a similar but more extreme manifesto, was the DDR. The fact that this party did not die in infancy suggested Jonny Kästner was a man with some qualities: idealistic, charismatic, a good organiser. His fatal flaw appears to have been that he thought one could make an omelette without breaking eggs."

"Not ruthless enough?"

"That's right. But lurking in the shadows of any extreme party you'll usually find people who *are* ruthless. If success suddenly appears possible, but there's a barrier to further progress, they may become impatient, and eventually take action."

"Which is why Breitling had Jonny Kästner killed."

"We believe so. Although we can't prove it."

"But why also kill Josie? If that's what has happened. Very risky and bound to bring unwelcome attention on themselves."

"I said Jonny Kästner must have been a good organiser to have kept his party alive for so long," replied Fischer. "In fact, we believe this was almost entirely due to his wife. It's a mistake to judge people by appearances. With all those tattoos and body piercings, Josie may have looked the classic hippy, but she was clearly a formidable back-room operator. Knew more about the DDR – and where the skeletons were buried

– than anyone else. Including Werner Breitling. That was bad enough; even worse was that people change. Josie in her thirties was a different person from the youngster who helped Jonny give birth to the party."

"She wanted to jump ship? Leave the DDR?"

"I believe the threat was much greater. She wanted to take the party along a different route from the one Werner had in mind. She was rebelling against his favourite tools: violence and intimidation."

"So you think Feldmann has killed Josie on Breitling's orders?"

The Chief Inspector hesitated. Finally: "It seems the most likely reason for her disappearance."

"Why has Feldmann also vanished?"

"Pretty obvious. With this second killing – if that's what it is – the finger of blame will be pointing firmly in his direction. He needs to slip beneath the radar for a while. Until people hopefully forget."

"I presume you've put out a missing persons search?"

"Of course." Fischer sounded quite offended. "But the two of them were last seen in Hungary, where my influence is, to say the least, limited. I've told my Budapest colleagues what we think, but don't hold your breath."

I thanked Fischer for his time and rang off. Went to the 'comfort' station to get rid of some of that coffee. Returned to my silver Porsche. Tried to work out what the devil I was going to say to young Karl.

Twenty-Eight

Traffic through the Czech Republic had been relatively benign and I made good progress; was well into Germany, the other side of Dresden and heading for Leipzig, when a sign caught my eye: 'Colditz'. Although this was somewhat out of my way, I was a sucker for escape films. I was close enough to my destination to be able to make it easily the next day and could do with some innocent amusement. Karl and the Harz Witch would have to wait a little longer.

I turned off the autobahn and twenty minutes later parked in the centre of Colditz, with the famous castle, which had held the most escape-crazy wartime prisoners, up there on the hill. I was too late for anything that day so booked a place on next morning's 10.30 tour: cash only, no plastic payment. The town's sleeping selection also left much to be desired; nearby I could only find a youth hostel and – call me a snob – did not fancy sharing a bunk with an acned eighteen-year-old. I eventually settled on a tolerable-looking hotel half a mile out of town.

I remembered Fischer's dictum that even now, over a quarter of a century after reunification, once off the beaten track you could still tell which towns had been dragged into the United Germany from former Stasiland; they were the ones with facilities below those of the west and a mindset that remained almost Soviet. Towns like Colditz.

Having found a bed for the night, I had work to do: take photos of the entries in Josie's diary for the coming six weeks and send them off to Fischer. The weather was sunny and warm, so I bought a half-litre Stein and went into their beer garden, armed with her diary. It felt strange to be Trudi-less; made me realise how lucky I'd been to find such a compatible travelling companion.

There are two types of diary: the backward-looking, which record the thoughts and events of that day for posterity; and the forward-looking, which are memory-joggers for the future. Josie's was a memory-jogger.

I went through it quickly, to see if anything obvious jumped out at me. There was nothing specific, but I could discern a pattern. Because pocket diaries have limited space, Josie, like most of us, used a shorthand. 'W' must surely stand for Werner, a letter that appeared with great regularity at the bottom of the page (bedtime!) during the earlier months, when Jonny had taken himself off to Dresden, but before he met his untimely end. The 'W's ended abruptly soon after the funeral, when Josie began to realise what her bed-mate might have been up to. Yes, 'W' must be Werner.

Later, several days were blocked off, with 'Frank Mohacs' written in. We knew all about that. But looking ahead, the part we were most interested in, the pages were mostly blank; just the odd birthday and dentist's visit. So the single word 'Königstein' looked naked as it stood there under 23rd September. Except it had been crossed out. A little further on I came to 30th September, which had just one large 'K'; reasonable to assume that 'Königstein' had been postponed for a week and was now identified by the single letter 'K'. I hadn't the faintest idea what that might signify; maybe it would mean something to Fischer.

As requested, I took photos of the largely uninteresting forward pages, then added four weeks from the past for reference. Sent the lot off to Fischer, with a short explanation.

My hotel did a better-than-expected dinner and afterwards produced a mattress to die for. Which I did. Even without Trudi.

Twenty-Nine

Next morning I went on the one-hour Colditz castle tour, regretting I couldn't afford the time for a longer version. Escapology is a never-ending fascination. But Karl and the Harz Witch were still about three hours away and I wanted to be back with the lad at the Lindtner in time for dinner.

I was about to speed off in my silver Porsche when my mobile rang. It was Chief Inspector Fischer, thanking me for the diary pictures.

"Not a lot there," I said.

"No… The word Königstein might mean something. To do with the castle, I expect. We'll bring some of our brains to bear on it…"

He paused. I waited.

"I've been thinking…"

I felt like being sarcastic, saying 'Not a bad idea to think', but bit my tongue. Waited some more.

Finally: "I think you should have a chat with Breitling."

I was taken aback. "Why? I've only met him once. Briefly at that. When he was spending his nights with Josie and opened the door to me as I delivered Karl back. He made it plain I wasn't welcome. And the feeling was mutual. What reason would I have to see him now?"

"The most obvious reason in the world. You find yourself landed with Josie's son and are wondering where she is. Wondering what's going on. As Josie's boss and lover – okay, ex-lover – he'd find it odd if you *didn't* want to see him."

I understood his logic, but hated the idea. I said: "So you want me to drop in on Werner, tell him we know he had Jonny Kästner bumped off and has now done the same with his wife. Yeah, we'd get on fine!"

Fischer gave me a moment to simmer down, then said: "You know what I mean, Ed. Pay Werner a visit. Naturally, you're worried. You don't know what to do with Karl, who's not *your* son, not *your* responsibility. See if *he* will look after the boy. I'll be willing to bet he won't."

I *was* simmering down; starting to realise that a visit to Herr Breitling might, after all, be an interesting challenge. So I said: "Okay. Maybe I will. I presume he's back in Dresden full time?"

"Lives above the office. Moved in when he became leader. Like most of its kind, the DDR is not flush with cash, so you'll find it's a modest establishment. Some would say squalid. I'll email you the address."

As I resumed my journey to fetch Karl, I realised I had made yet another commitment; allowed myself to sink even deeper into the morass of German right-wing politics.

Thirty

'Mountains' is usually the word used to describe the Harz, but in fact it's not much more than an undulating plateau rising about 1,000 metres above the north German plain; a mix of forest, farmland and defunct mining industries.

During the Cold War it had been border country – the Iron Curtain running down the middle: Federal Republic of Germany on one side, Stasiland on the other. Separating the two was a death strip of barbed wire, mines and goon towers, designed to stop anyone in the East leaving their workers' paradise.

This old border is now the preserve of ramblers and amateur historians; as a brown roadside sign with a map of Europe explained: 'Here Germany and Europe were divided until 14.30 on 12th November 1989'. I liked the precise timing. Next to it was a grey stone memorial with the inscription: 'Germany. United again'. Rather moving.

A couple of miles after this old border, I rolled into Braunlage, once the West's last outpost before the Badlands. I paused at the downtown T-junction. Riding the tiles of a house over to the left was a witch astride her broomstick, so I had to be in the right place. Straight ahead were a couple of shops with garish signs: 'Wagner's Bakery', with oversized depictions of his products; and 'The Little Magic World' for kids. In an odd way it reminded me of Blackpool. No tower or beach, but there was the same air of quiet desperation, an attempt to market 1930s fun in the 21st century. Braunlage's glory days had been between the wars, before mass travel had been invented; but now skiers can find better snow and steeper slopes in the Alps, while in summer it's off to the Med or further afield. The Harz is yesterday's destination.

But not for hard-up parents seeking a cheap way of getting youngsters off their hands for a couple of weeks. It remained summer camp territory. My Satnav sent me left at the T-junction, past the church, then down a side road. In front of a well-kept detached house, circa 1930, with floral window boxes, it told me I had arrived. So I stopped, got out and rang the doorbell.

"Hi!"

From my phone call I'd been expecting a witch. But the vision of loveliness that stood before me… I was spellbound. She could have been from one of those Leni Riefenstahl films that glorified Nazi maidens – after all, this *was* time-warp town. Riefenstahl, who died not that long ago aged 101, had been Hitler's great buddy and propagandist. In her movies, all the girls had been blonde, slim and Aryan. And gorgeous.

The vision smiled and said: "Sorry if I was rather short with you over the phone. To be honest, I was getting worried. I love doing summer camp, but can't keep the kids for ever."

She was my 'witch', no question. Same voice. Just showed one should never judge sight by sound. I was saved further awkwardness by the arrival of a tornado – Karl, clutching a small bag.

"Hi there, big boy! Had a good time?" I ruffled his hair.

He looked up, nodded, half shy. I was familiar, but not *that* familiar.

"Say thank you to the nice lady". I didn't know her name and could hardly call her the witch.

Karl offered a formal handshake and received a hug in return.

"My regards to Frau Kästner," said the lovely witch, as she waved us goodbye.

I managed a nod and a smile. But wished she hadn't brought up the subject. Karl was bound to start asking questions about his mother. What the hell was I supposed to tell him?

Thirty-One

To my astonishment and relief, Karl seemed less interested in his mother than the electronic gizmo in his hand. Years ago, when I'd had children of his age, holiday departures had been a trial of strength between the generations. The kick-off question, five minutes after leaving our own drive, had always been 'When will we be there?', to which our answer had always been 'soon', even though we might have had eight hours ahead of us. As Karl's littler fingers danced across his tablet, I realised journeys could now last forever for all they cared.

We were putting the last of the Harz behind us – the signposts said 'Blankenburg' – when I could stand the tension no longer. Casually, I said:

"When we get home, you'll be staying at Frau Lindtner's for a while."

"I know. Mum said." This without a pause in his finger-dance.

"When did your mother tell you?"

Another long pause while he negotiated a tricky phase of his game. Then: "Dunno."

"Did she say when she'll collect you?" I persisted. "How long will you be staying with us?"

"Not long. Until she's finished."

"Finished what?"

"Dunno."

His lack of any sense of time was infuriating. Josie had not been seen for over a week, yet her son was behaving as though they had recently been in touch. Was that possible?

The rest of the drive back was conducted in silence. My imagination continued working overtime, without coming to any conclusion. When we finally drew up outside the Hotel Lindtner, the Kästner puzzle was put on hold by a domestic drama: Trudi's daughter Birgit, the hotel's new manager, had flounced off in a huff.

First we got Karl fed and put to bed. Tomorrow it was back to school, which would relieve us of a chunk of parenting time. Later, when the last of the guests had finished dinner, Trudi let the waiter go, locked the dining room door and fetched the Jägermeister. Just like old times.

"What happened?" I asked.

She shook her head sadly. "My fault, I suppose. When I got back I was quite upset. So many things were no longer like the *old* Lindtner. I like to run a slick ship, not over-fussy but efficient. I hate to say anything against my own daughter, but…"

"You *did* say something?"

Trudi nodded. "We both did. Became quite heated. And unpleasant."

"So she walked out?"

"There was probably more to it. She has a new boyfriend, who helps his father run a garage in Pirna. Seems a nice lad, the little I saw of him. I think Birgit has had enough of hotels and wants to try something else – with *someone* else. Our bust-up may have been merely an excuse"

"Leaving you back at the grindstone."

She gave a little smile. "I'm almost relieved. Don't get me wrong; I've had a wonderful summer, loved every minute. But now it's back to normal and I need something to do. I'm not the sort to spend my time in the back room eating chocolates."

"Remember, you're now lumbered with a new family: Karl will have to live *somewhere*."

"He hasn't said anything that might give us a clue as to what's happened to his mother?"

"Can't make him out," I replied. "He doesn't *seem* bothered that his mother's not around, but that may be just a defence mechanism; a refusal to believe something that's too ghastly to believe. But I don't think so. The boy appears to be... if not exactly happy, at least content. As though this is a slightly annoying episode he knows won't last too long."

"Do *you* have any new ideas about Josie?"

I shook my head. "I've given up trying."

"Well, Karl's welcome to stay, at least for a while." Trudi took a sip of Jägermeister. "But then we have *you* to consider ."

"Me?" I feigned surprise, pretty sure we'd both been thinking along similar lines.

"You appear on my doorstep in early summer, telling me you're doing Europe. Then you fall foul of our mafia. And I..." she grinned "...I allow myself to be seduced. Become your floozy in exile. But now summer's over and it's back to normal. So what are your plans? Will you be returning to that wife of yours in England?"

"Heaven forbid! I couldn't face any more of Maggie. Besides, we're officially divorced."

"What then? You won't want to stay here... will you?"

I'd been trying to push this problem to the back of my mind. Although I'd signed away my marital home, I could perhaps return to the UK, rent an apartment, and try some consultancy work. An unattractive prospect.

The trouble with escapism is that one day you have to come back to earth. However, I felt there was still some life left in my present jaunt and replied:

""You may have to put up with me a little longer because I still have work to do for Chief Inspector Fischer. He wants me to brave the Breitling ogre in his den. See how he reacts."

"What good will that do?"

I shrugged. "Don't know. Remember he lived with Josie for a while. Karl even called him 'Uncle Werner'. He'd think it odd if I did *not* come knocking on his door with questions about Josie."

"If he *is* in any way responsible, he's not going to admit it."

"No, but I might learn something. Get a feel for things."

"I suppose…" Trudi did not sound convinced. "But meanwhile, it's back to the old routine. Which means it's bedtime."

I smiled and followed her into the servants' quarter; a little more of the 'the old routine' would not be too painful.

Thirty-Two

It took three days to arrange my assignation with the leader of the German Democratic Right. My first thought had been to simply turn up, but that might have led to rejection and hardened his heart to *never* see me. So I had gone through the proper channels, phoned and stated my business. My reward was an appointment with the great man at 2.30pm.

Although I'd spent most of the summer exploring Europe, I'd missed out on my doorstep destination, Dresden. I'd driven the motorway round the city and been kidnapped by Inspector Kirst to his police station somewhere in the northern suburbs, but that was it.

Dresden is a name that provokes a reaction. It wasn't so much its destruction, which was par for the course for German cities during the war, rather that the destruction was arguably needless. By February 1945 the Third Reich was little more than a smouldering ruin, but medieval Dresden was still intact.

Then, with the conflict almost over, allied bombers ensured that also this city shared the fate of the others. Necessary or not? Historians will forever dispute the point.

I had visited Dresden once before, during my frustrating but fascinating youthful foray into what was then the German Democratic Republic – Stasiland. The Communists had made *some* efforts to repair the damage, bringing Zwinger Palace and Semper Opera back to their former glory. But then the usual lethargy had set in, so that the old town's most iconic monument, the Frauenkirche, still lay on the ground in numbered fragments; a pathetic jigsaw, which someone, someday, might get around to re-assembling.

The years of Communist neglect had been quickly remedied by the Unified Germany, so now everyone can enjoy one of Europe's great vistas: the River Elbe with the restored Frauenkirche as its centrepiece.

The Dresden of Werner Breitling lay behind this facade, in one of the huge blocks put up in haste after the war to get roofs over heads. Perhaps I should not be too hard on Stasiland. Mention St. Paul's post-war Paternoster Square to any Londoner and he'll cringe in shame; the '60s and '70s were decades of architectural vandalism world-wide, the only difference being that the Reds managed to build even nastier than the West.

I made no attempt at old-fashioned navigation, just set up my Satnav and obeyed orders, which brought me to a Soviet-style block… somewhere in Dresden. A ground-floor sign read 'German Democratic Right'. Beside it was a half-open door, a democratic enough invitation, so in I went.

The office girl was about the same age as Josie, but had mouse-blonde hair that was uncoloured; and no painted or pierced flesh. She recognised my name and invited me to sit down, on the single, metal chair, adding: "The leader will see you in a moment."

In German there are two options for the word 'leader': 'Führer' or 'Leiter'. Breitling was their 'Leiter'. During my travels I never came across a leader that was a 'Führer'; nor met any man called Adolf. Words erased by history.

It was a poky office, with a few filing cabinets, a desk with a landline phone and mobile, and political posters around the walls. I was amused by one of these, a 'DDR Happy Family' advert, which featured a younger Karl beside a blonde girl and with different parents. Why had Jonny excluded himself from this piece of publicity? And had Josie been deemed not sufficiently photogenic?

The minutes ticked by. I glanced at my watch: 2.40. Those who fancy themselves as 'leaders' always make the great unwashed wait. At 2.45 a door opened and a large head attached to an equally impressive neck appeared.

"Herr Blake, do come in. Sorry to have kept you."

The head was shaved on top, with a couple of days' growth beneath. The face in between smiled. Unlike our previous meeting, when I had returned Karl to Josie, Werner Breitling was making an effort to be nice.

The DDR's 'Leiter' was a large man in every sense and had a reputation – at least with the police and me – as a thug. But in his neat blue trousers and crisp white shirt he looked more like a successful executive. As the public face of one of Germany's more notorious organisations, he had been carefully crafted to not frighten the children.

He indicated the spare chair – more comfortable than the one in his anteroom. I sat down, while he took up his command position behind a desk. Eyed me questioningly.

"You can probably guess why I'm here," I began. "I've just fetched Karl from summer camp, apparently at the request of his mother. But she seems to have disappeared. Any idea where she might be?"

"As you know, Josie was doing a little job for me in Hungary…"

So word had got back to Werner that I had been there; in spite of Josie's initial efforts to keep this quiet.

"She'd been working hard – too hard maybe – so I suggested she took some time off. I expect she's decided to see more of Hungary; a delightful country."

"She vanished from the guesthouse we were staying in," I pointed out. "Taking the owner's pet dog, but leaving her own car behind. Pretty weird, you must admit."

"Had she paid her bill?"

"Yes…"

"There you are! She's just enjoying a well-earned rest and, being a poor driver, has decided not to use her car. People have been known to take trains and buses."

"And Frau Molnar's Rottweiler?"

"Really, Herr Blake…" Breitling waved a dismissive hand. "…Dogs are forever getting out… escaping. Nothing to do with Josie. You've been seeing too many TV movies."

I continued doggedly (no pun intended): "There's also the fact that one of your employees, Josef Feldmann, visited Frau Kästner shortly before she disappeared."

"Careful how you use that word 'fact', Herr Blake." Breitling's friendly mask was slipping. "It's *not* a fact that Feldmann is employed either by me or the party. He helps out, does odd job for me. Nothing more. Neither is it a *fact* that he visited Josie in Hungary."

"Frau Molnar opened the door to the man, so she got a good look. I showed her a photo of Feldmann and she's sure it was him."

Breitling shook his head sadly. Mockingly. "Maybe you *should* watch some of those TV movies. Then you'd know that so-called identifications are hopelessly unreliable. Show that witness of yours a picture of King Kong and she'd still swear it was Feldmann."

I felt I was losing the argument, so in desperation asked: "I'm told Feldmann has not been seen around here for a while. Where do *you* think he is?"

As if talking to an especially dim child, Breitling replied: "You're not listening, Herr Blake: I said Josef Feldmann is *not* in my employ. Sure, he can be seen around the office from time to time, but he's his own master. Can do what he likes. I have no *idea* where he is. Or what he's doing. Just like the other millions who live around Dresden."

I played my final card: "Well, someone will have to do something about young Karl. If Josie does not return…"

"Of course she'll return!"

I was not to be put off: "…If his mother does not come back, Frau Lindtner can't be expected to look after the lad forever. He used to call you 'Uncle Werner', so…"

Breitling gave a guffaw, slapped his thigh: "Good try, Herr Blake. I'll give you that. But you know full well I'm just an honorary uncle, not a real one. And my arrangement with Frau Kästner was merely temporary. I like young Karl, a nice boy; but to be brutally honest, he's absolutely nothing to do with me."

"Then what will become of him if Josie never returns?"

"*Of course* she'll return. But if, by some strange chance, this merry widow on the loose meets a handsome young devil, what can the rest of us do about it?"

"In that case I have no doubt Frau Kästner will make the necessary arrangements. But what if she has met with an accident? Is unable to take care of her son?"

The remaining remnants of Breitling's phoney good humour vanished. Quietly, he asked: "What do you mean by that?"

For a crazy moment I felt like replying 'We think you arranged to have both the Kästners killed'. But I lost my nerve. Common sense took over. I merely shrugged and mumbled: "Well… you know… accidents can happen."

"Breitling gave a half-smile, as though guessing my cowardice. Said: "If this preposterous theory of yours does come to pass and Josie fails to return, I pay a fortune in taxes to make sure everyone in Germany has a safety net. Social Security will take good care of her son."

I nodded, dumbly. There was a moment's silence. Then, with a smug smile, Werner Breitling asked: "Was there anything else, Herr Blake?"

I had meant to quiz him about his party and politics, but the fight had gone out of me. I felt like a rookie boxer after ten rounds against the champ. I just thanked the 'Leiter' for his time and departed with as much dignity as I could muster.

Thirty-Three

It was not a happy Herr Blake that sat down with his employer for their routine post-dinner chat. I don't like being humiliated, which had been my fate at the hands of Werner Breitling.

The infuriating thing was that his comments had been perfectly logical. Josie *could* be taking a break without telling us; the fact that Karl seemed quite unconcerned suggested that he knew mum was okay.

Dogs *did* escape; there was not a shred of evidence to support our theory that this had anything to do with Josie.

And Frau Molnar's 'confirmation' that Josie's visitor had been Feldmann could well be because I had predisposed her to give this reply. My case against Breitling had been built on shifting sand.

"Anyway, Karl seems to be settling down," said Trudi, in an effort to inject some positive thinking. "He can walk to school from here and is back with all his old pals. Doesn't seem at all put out that his mother is not around."

"Are *you* happy to be back at the hotel?"

Trudi smiled. "It may sound ungrateful, but I've never been happier. Franz died… what is it?… over twenty years ago, and in that time I've hardly had a day away from here. I needed a break. Which you, lovely man, have given me. But I'm now back, with a full tank of fuel…"

"Ready for another twenty years?"

"Maybe not that long…"

"What about Birgit? How is she taking it?"

"Many youngsters don't really know what they want to do with their lives; have to experiment. I think Birgit *had to* give it a go: try running the hotel on her own. It didn't work out. Then along comes this new boyfriend, with whom she seems suitably besotted… Just hope *that* works out. Birgit would make someone an excellent wife."

"Say anything like that in public and you'll be lynched. Remember, this is the age of feminism, when every gal must have a career."

Trudi smiled. "But we're the dinosaur age; can say what we like. No one takes any notice."

I gave her a kiss. A couple of dinosaurs, late at night in an empty hotel dining room.

Trudi sat back. With a wry smile said: "Our only problem seems to be a stray Englishman. What should we do with him?"

What indeed! I had thought of little else. I had nothing to go back to in England, yet my summer adventure was clearly at an end. Autumn was upon us and this season is usually followed by winter. I had been so keen to sever the knot tying me to Maggie that I had launched myself into space with little thought about any long-term future. I had plenty of money and hopefully a few years left in the bank, but how to spend them I had no idea.

"Of course, you can stay here as long as you like," said Trudi. "Until you've made up your mind. Usual deal, help in the hotel and keep me happy. As you also don't need paying, I can't believe my luck."

I nodded slowly. "There are still a lot of loose ends. Who killed Jonny Kästner? What's happened to Josie? And the Feldmann enigma. I'd like to see some of these resolved. So yes, I'll hang around for a while. Let's say at least until that mysterious entry in Josie's diary: 'Königstein, 30th September'. Must mean something."

Thirty-Four

Ten days later, nicely settled into the old routine, I received a phone call from Chief Inspector Fischer. Josie's diary and the report on my fiasco with Breitling had gone off to him within the day, stereotyped emails received in return, so I was hoping he might be the bearer of some proper news.

It was not to be. He started off with 'Ed', rather than 'Mr. Blake', heralding a casual chat. He said the Chemnitz riots and their aftermath had been dealt with, there was nothing new on the Kästner killing and his other cases were non-urgent. He could afford to take a breather.

In Fischer's dictionary, 'breather' merely meant that he added a dollop of pleasure to his work; threw some ideas around, chewed the cud. Would our usual trysting place, the Restaurant am Fluss, be okay?

After consulting the boss I was able to agree the following evening at 7.30. Although halfway through September, continental Europe still retained much of its summer heat, so we were able to sit out on the terrace, only about three-quarters full now that the main season was over. To my right was the grassy flood plain, where Jonny, Karl and I had aimlessly kicked a ball around. Where, some three months ago, it had all started

The Chief Inspector was nattily dressed in light brown slacks and blue pullover, as usual looking too young for his rank. I suspected he wanted my company more to practise his English than discuss the case, so before starting on the serious stuff, I asked:

"Have you spent much time in England? Your accent is excellent. Could almost take you for a native."

He smiled at the compliment, then replied: "Not been to the UK as much as I'd have liked. But I *was* lucky enough to be selected for a course at Bramshill."

He paused. I looked blank. He explained: "Bramshill, the police college. Near Basingstoke in Hampshire. Old Jacobean house, with stained-glass windows, heraldic shields on the walls, cellar large enough to store wine for an entire army. Even a resident ghost."

"Doesn't sound very suitable for a college – police or otherwise."

"It wasn't. Must have cost a fortune to run – especially to heat in winter. Which is probably why it's no longer a police college. A pity, because it had oodles of atmosphere."

'Oodles'; not many non-Brits would have dug out a word like that.

I said: "And now you're having to deal with an errant Englishman who's strayed onto your patch in Germany."

He nodded, took a sip of wine – he'd chosen a local Gold Riesling, from Meissen – and said: "I suggested this meeting because the Kästner case is bugging me. Not only because we've had no result and little prospect of getting one, but also on account of that date in Josie's diary. 30th September. Less than two weeks away. We still have no idea what it might mean."

"*Königstein* on 30th September," I stressed. "Does your team have any thoughts on the name?"

He shook his head. "The castle, obviously. Or the town. Something due to happen there. But what? We have no clues."

"Sorry I can't help," I said. "I *did* have a few ideas, but these have been demolished by Breitling. Rightly so, I'm afraid."

"Yes, Breitling," Fischer latched onto the name. "You say he gave you a bad time, but what else can you tell me about him? What was your impression?"

"Large, aggressive, not to be trifled with."

"I ask, because his party, the DDR, is producing a lot of electronic activity," said Fischer. "Too much, we think, to be day-to-day stuff. Looks like they're planning something. And that worries us."

"What do you mean by electronic activity?"

"Emails and text messages. Mostly between Breitling and Feldmann."

"Feldmann!" I was astonished. "I thought he'd disappeared. Like Josie."

"We may not know *where* he is, but he's certainly around somewhere. He and Werner are communicating like young lovers."

"Saying what?"

"That's the problem. They have a private… not so much a code as an understanding. For example, they might use the word 'Lorelei' to refer to Dresden. And their messages tend to be very short, just a few characters. Probably only confirmations or not about something in the pipeline."

"Surely you can track these calls?"

"Of course. Breitling's almost always come from his Dresden office, or nearby. Feldmann's have come from all over the place: Hungary while you were there…"

"You *knew* Feldmann was in Visegrad at the same time as Josie?" I was furious. "Had *I* known that, I could have scored at least one point against Breitling, who rubbished the whole notion of Feldmann being in Hungary."

Fischer was unperturbed by my outburst; continued to dissect his trout like a master surgeon. Finally: "Sorry about that. We don't want Breitling to know that *you* know what *we* know – if you see what I mean."

I did see. Although I was still miffed I let it pass and asked: "You say Feldmann has been phoning from all over the place. Where, apart from Hungary?"

"Various places around Berlin."

"Berlin! What the devil is he doing there?"

"Lying low, I imagine. It's where he was born and spent his younger days. If our theory that Feldmann killed both the Kästners is correct, he won't want to be seen anywhere near Dresden."

"But he still needs to be in contact with headquarters."

"Yes. If, as I fear, they are hatching something. But they only use text messages, no voice, and Feldmann always turns his phone off after each contact. We can't track inert phones, so we have a map of Berlin with little spots showing places he called from. Nothing in between. Nothing to tell us where he might be living. Frustrating."

"This man, Feldmann," I said. "Only met him that once; on the boat when I stumbled across Kästner's body. What's his background?"

"Like I said, born in Berlin. Forty-three years ago to a seventeen-year-old prostitute. Father unknown."

"Not a great start in life."

"It doesn't get any better, because he grew up in care homes and with various short-term foster parents. Almost inevitable that as an adult he'd fall in with a bad lot: petty crime, bit of drug pushing, but at that stage nothing too vicious. Arrested twice, but never charged. Between odd jobs he relied mainly on state handouts, junk food and plenty of beer."

"Hence the beer gut."

Fischer nodded. "No one could accuse Feldmann of being a fit man. Then, about three years ago, he was 'rescued', if I can put it like that, by the DDR, who made him their unofficial office boy and – to the outside world at least – put him on the straight and narrow."

"Except that Werner gives him the job of killing Kästner."

Fischer nodded. "When we looked into how Feldmann got that job with the Saxon Steamship Company, the man who recommended him was…"

"Breitling!"

"Exactly. Feldmann owes everything to Breitling and now the two of them are up to something. I can almost smell it…" the Chief Inspector was more agitated than I'd ever seen him. "…I don't know what the hell it is, but that date, 30th September *must* mean something."

"Is there anything I can do?"

Fischer shook his head. Shrugged. "Probably not. But I need all my troops on standby, in case…"

"So *I've* been recruited into your army?"

He grinned. "Have been for months. To begin with you were a conscript; remember, we insisted you stay. Then you became a volunteer. Saw action in Hungary, for which we're most grateful. I hope you'll remain with the colours a little longer: at least until that niggling date has come and gone."

I nodded. "I'd planned to do that anyway. Loose ends. I hate them."

"Good man." Chief Inspector Fischer clapped me on the shoulder. As Commanding Officers went, I could do a lot worse.

Thirty-Five

My mobile rang at 7.10am. Not a time of day that usually brings good news. Trudi stirred beside me, unwilling to wake up. Although Lindtner breakfasts started at 7am, they were buffet affairs, usually supervised by one of the girls, allowing madam a well-earned lie-in. I slipped out of bed, into the bathroom and shut the door.

"Yes?"

"Sorry to call so early. Hope I didn't wake you." It was Chief Inspector Fischer."

"I believe I'm awake. Just."

"There's been a development…" An ominous word, 'development'.

As I did not respond, he continued: "I didn't want to call you until we had definite news, but for the past few days we've been talking to our friends in Budapest…"

My heart sank: "You mean Josie?"

"…A man was walking his dog over rough ground not far from the Visegrad royal palace, when the animal became excited; started yelping and pawing the ground. Turned out to be a shallow and hastily dug grave…"

"Oh no!" I should never have allowed Josie to go off on her own. It was all my fault.

"The Hungarian forensic team soon discovered it was not one grave, but two, lying side by side," continued Fischer remorselessly. "The smaller of the two contained a large dog…"

"Attila!"

"Belonging to a Mrs. Molnar. That was comparatively easy to establish. The human remains proved more difficult, having been in the ground some time and suffering a degree of… er… deterioration."

"There was nothing to say who she was?" I assumed it was Josie.

"The site had been deliberately stripped of everything that would lead to easy identification, but the clothing suggested someone who was not Hungarian, probably German. Which is when they brought me in. It has taken a few days, but dental records have proved conclusive. The human remains have been confirmed as being those of a middle-aged man…"

"…Did you say 'man'?"

"Positively identified as Josef Feldmann."

My head was in a whirl.

I blurted out: "Feldmann? Are you sure?"

"Science does not lie."

"If Feldmann is dead, who sent all those texts from Berlin, using his phone?"

"There's only one possible answer."

"Josie Kästner!"

"Of course."

"If Feldmann is dead and Josie still missing…" My carefully assembled jigsaw had been scattered on the ground, leaving me to start again from scratch. But I might be able to fit one piece, so asked: "Attila was known to react violently to Feldmann. Was he killed by the dog?"

"According to the autopsy, Feldmann had suffered severe neck and head wounds, almost certainly from the Rottweiler," replied Fischer. "But what actually killed him was a sequence of knife thrusts."

"Like Jonny Kästner."

"Similar sort of knife maybe, but otherwise very different. Jonny Kästner died from a single clinical stab: a professional job. Feldmann's death was caused by a frenzy of multiple blows. Unlikely to be the same killer. And we *don't* believe Josie murdered her husband."

"But she *did* kill Feldmann?"

"Almost certainly. With passion. The only other suspect might be the dog's owner, Mrs. Molnar."

"That's absurd."

"They say she was very fond of her pet. If she discovered Feldmann had killed him, she *might* have resorted to violence."

"With a knife? You've never met the lady, but I have. She's elderly, placid, wouldn't say boo to a goose. She *might* have resorted to beating Feldmann on the chest; more likely she'd simply collapse in a heap. Anyway, why would she be wandering around with a knife?"

"You're right, of course. The Hungarian police interviewed Mrs. Molnar as their first suspect, but she insisted Attila had simply vanished – probably released by one of her guests. That's all she knew. It soon became obvious she was telling the truth. So they let her go."

I said: "So it has to be Josie. I suppose there'll be a warrant out for her arrest."

There was a pause. For a moment, I thought Fischer had hung up. Then he said: "What I tell you now must remain between ourselves. If we can locate her, Josie Kästner will one day be questioned about her part – if any – in the death of Josef Feldmann. That's the law. But I'm not Inspector Kirst, who works for the Saxony State police. Nor do I have any connection with Hungary, where the crime took place. My loyalty is to the German Federal Government's Anti-Extremism Bureau. I strongly suspect that the German Democratic Right is planning something. Our only asset in their secretive world is Josie Kästner. We want her to remain at large, not rotting in a cell undergoing a criminal investigation. At least, not until the current situation has been resolved."

"What happens now?" I was feeling punch-drunk from these latest developments.

"Fortunately, the Hungarian police are not in possession of all the facts. They only know that Feldmann checked in to the Visegrad hotel and later knocked on Mrs. Molnar's door, enquiring about one of her guests. During the course of that visit, which, according to her lasted only a few seconds, her faithful hound Attila, usually the most amenable of animals, went crazy at his presence."

"Did Frau Molnar mention *which* guest he was looking for?"

"Says she can't remember. Donaublick gets hundreds of guests every season and this was weeks ago."

"That's nonsense," I said.

"Of course it is. But the Rottweiler was like a child to Molnar; she'd want to protect anyone who might have avenged his death; someone like Josie, with whom she'd already built up a good relationship."

"So the Hungarian police are unaware of the connection between Feldmann and Josie?"

"Hopefully, their only clue will remain the list of names for the day in question in Molnar's guest book. Could be any of half a dozen people."

"But if they started digging deeper into that half dozen?"

"I've sent them a diversion," said Fischer breezily. "The Hungarian police now have a file, a kilometre long, on Feldmann's misdeeds. Doesn't make pretty reading. I've hinted at a mafia killing; a falling out amongst the criminal fraternity. With luck, they'll start chasing those leads. Which should buy us enough time for Josie to deliver any goods she may have."

I could hear Trudi noises from next door so said: "Madam's on the march. I'll give her the good news about Josie. So thanks for calling and…"

"Woah, woah! Don't ring off. I have a job for you."

"A job? For *me*?"

You're in my army, remember? Or have you resigned your commission?"

"No, no. 'Course not. What do you want me to do?"

"It's not so much for me as Mrs. Molnar. So far she has kept commendably silent. But when I had a few words with her over the phone, she said she was prepared to talk. But only to you. Only to Mr. Blake in person."

"She won't take a phone call?"

"She said not. Phones can be tapped, bugged, etcetera. If that sounds paranoid, remember her normal humdrum life has been shattered by those corpses in the wood. Anyway, that's her condition."

"You want me to drive all the way back to Visegrad?"

"Please."

"When?"

"Within the hour would be good."

Thirty-Six

My bathroom phone call had woken Trudi, who was now half dressed. I repeated Fischer's story, to which her reaction was "Thank God Josie is okay."

I pointed out that Josie was still missing, her safety still uncertain. Frau Molnar might have some of the answers we needed, so I'd be off after a quick breakfast. Count me out for any Lindtner work during the next few days.

Google informed me the distance to Visegrad was 683 kilometres and would take 7 hours 13 minutes. If my silver Porsche was feeling frisky, I might shave a few minutes off that; on the other hand, roadworks and traffic could have the opposite effect. I rang Frau Molnar and told her I hoped to be there by dinner time.

I'm one of those heretics who believes Satnav is not infallible and should be tempered by common sense, so it was a help that my route between Saxony and the Danube Bend was becoming quite familiar. Now I could edge towards that correct but badly signed lane in plenty of time; and I knew when those unexpected turns were coming up. I had a snack at a motorway service station the other side of Prague and rolled into Visegrad just after 5.30pm.

My welcome was a tearful hug, a far cry from the self-possessed Molnar of previous visits. When I started asking questions, she quickly shut me up with 'Later'; didn't want to discuss *anything* in her house. We'd talk somewhere else; over dinner.

She seemed nervous enough to believe any sort of nonsense, even that her own house might have been bugged. It was not for me to argue, so after her guests for the night had checked in, I piled her into the Porsche and headed for our old 'Etterem' on the Danube.

Frau Molnar had dressed up for the occasion, a nice little number that was probably fashionable in the 1970s. She was not averse to a mild stimulant, so I ordered a full bottle of the local Neszmély white.

It seemed to do the trick, so after ten minutes or so I said: "Are you ready to tell me what happened?"

She leant forward, intensely: "You must tell *no one*. Understand?"

I nodded.

"Except, of course, your lovely wife."

Wife? Ah… must mean Trudi. Frau Molnar came from the generation when every couple venturing abroad was assumed to be legally united.

"Absolutely no one must know what I'll be telling you," she insisted. "That includes the police. *Especially* not the police."

"Not a soul," I assured her. Then, for a moment abandoning German for English: "Cross my heart and hope to die."

Her English wasn't up to much, but she got the message. Managed a feeble smile.

"You know how it started," she began. "That man rang the doorbell… it was quite early, still light, so maybe 6.30pm Almost at once Attila started howling. He is – was – a very good judge of character; knew who he liked and who he didn't. Never got it wrong, so the visitor had to be a bad 'un.

"He asked for Frau Kästner. I wasn't at all happy about it, but what could I do? So I called Josie and they talked for maybe a couple of minutes. Then I heard the front door close. Attila stopped barking and I thought no more about it.

"I don't go out much these days; usually cook myself dinner and sit down to watch the telly. Then early to bed with a good book. So it can't have been late. I'd just put my dirty plates in the dishwasher when there was a banging on my door. This was *most* unusual. My guests have their own key to the front door as well as to their rooms, so there's no need to disturb me in my private apartment. As that front door is always locked, it *had* to be one of my guests, so I opened up."

"It was Josie?"

Frau Molnar nodded and gave a little shiver. "She looked *terrible*. Caked in mud – there'd been a lot of rain recently – but worst was the blood, all over her clothes, even in her hair. For a moment we just stood and stared at each other. Then she said: 'It was Attila. Please, you must help me.' I couldn't understand it: she and Attila had been such good friends. Then, realising what I must be thinking, she added: 'No, no, it wasn't *Attila's* fault. He *saved* me'.

"I hardly knew what I was doing. Put on a warm cardigan – by now it was dark and getting cold. Fetched a torch. Followed Josie out. Started walking towards the centre of town.

"I asked Josie what on earth she was thinking of, going out like that – *alone*? She replied they'd agreed to meet by the church, where it was well lit and she should be safe. As an added precaution, she'd taken Attila. But only a hundred metres from Donaublick, where the houses are well spread out, with trees and undergrowth just off the road, she'd been ambushed."

For some moments the old lady was unable to go on. I said nothing, re-filled her glass and waited. At last she continued:

"I still have nightmares. Josie led me off the road, only a few steps, into a small copse. There, under a tree…"

Again she faltered. I gave her some more recovery time, then prompted: "Under a tree…? Yes…?"

"It was that man. Josie's visitor. Dead. Horribly dead. Beside him, poor Attila. Both covered in blood. I asked Josie what had happened. She said the man had come up from behind and grabbed her round the neck. It was dark, like I said, so he can't have noticed Attila, but as soon as this happened Attila went for him."

Frau Molnar shook her head, as though trying to erase the memory. As she seemed disinclined to elaborate, I asked:

"Did Josie say how Attila died?"

Again she shook her head helplessly.

According to Fischer, Feldmann had first been mauled by the dog, then finished off with a knife, presumably wielded by Josie. But why was the dog also dead? Didn't make sense.

But Frau Molnar was in shock at having to re-live that awful night. She just sat there, unable or unwilling to answer my question.

I tried another tack: "So you helped Josie remove the bodies and bury them?"

The old lady nodded. "She told me we couldn't bury them there. It was too near a house, too close to town. Bound to be discovered. We'd have to take them away, to somewhere less obvious. Using *my* car, which wouldn't be so suspicious."

Josie was being remarkably clear headed. Any contamination of *her* car had to be avoided at all costs.

"So you went back, fetched your car and loaded the bodies into it," I said. "Who decided where to bury them?"

"I did, of course. I knew the area; eventually picked a spot, a kilometre or two out of town. Should have taken them further out, I realise that now, but at the time I couldn't face it. As it was, it took us ages; terribly hard work. I had just the one spade, which we took it in turns to use, but I'm no longer young and Josie is so small a puff of wind would blow her over."

I nodded in sympathy. She had still not answered that question about how Attila had come to be killed, so I put it differently:

"What do *you* think happened that night, Frau Molnar?"

She recoiled, confused. "I just told you. Poor Josie was attacked and Attila saved her. Those were her exact words: 'Attila saved me'."

To make sure I had her story correctly, I then asked: "And Attila killed that man?"

"Of course! Haven't I just said?"

I nodded absentmindedly, trying to work out what was going on. Molnar believed her dog had not only attacked Feldmann, but also killed him. No wonder she was nervous.

However, the *facts* were that her dog had only attacked Feldmann, not killed him. As Fischer put it, 'Science does not lie'. The fatal wounds had been caused by a knife. How had Attila come to die? The only person who could answer that was Josie Kästner.

I realised Frau Molnar had been speaking and I had not been paying attention. I apologised and asked her to repeat herself.

"Can they put me in prison for allowing my dog to kill someone?"

I almost replied that Attila had *not* killed Feldmann, then thought better of it. Better stick to the story Josie had spun. Instead I asked *her* a question:

"The police have interviewed you – right?"

She nodded. "It wasn't very pleasant."

"And you're quite clearly not in prison."

She stared at me, wondering where this was leading.

"If they were going to detain you, they'd already have done it," I assured her, with a confidence I did not feel.

"Besides…" I dropped my voice and gave her a conspiratorial look. "…I have it on good authority that the dead man was a wanted criminal. Had they been able, the police would probably have given Attila a medal."

"So he was a good dog?"

A very good dog."

My suggestion that her beloved Attila had done the right thing seemed to calm her. I took the opportunity to ask:

"The police only became involved a couple of days ago when the bodies were discovered. But going back to that night, what did you do when you'd finished burying them?"

"Drove home and cleaned my car. After that I took Josie to my apartment and poured us both a stiff drink. Josie said that in the morning I must report Attila missing. Nothing else. If they discovered the bodies, again I was to say *nothing*. I had to tell them I didn't know any Frau Kästner, apart from her being one of my many guests."

"So that's all you've told the police? That Atilla went missing."

"Of course!"

"What happened to Josie?"

"I don't know. She said she'd clean up, try to get some sleep and leave as planned the next morning. I thought she'd go as she'd come, by car, but next day her car was still sitting in my drive. She never turned up for breakfast, so must have taken an early bus. Anyway, I never saw her again."

"But you rang me to ask if I could remove her car."

Frau Molnar nodded. "Josie phoned a couple of days later. Apologised for leaving the car, but said it was safer that way; she had to disappear for a while and didn't want to leave any tracks. But if I wanted the car moved, I could ring you."

"Why *me*?"

"She felt we could trust you."

"But you said nothing to me about Feldmann being killed."

"Of course not. We were still hoping the bodies would never be found."

"Now they *have* been found, do you think she still trusts me?"

"Must do, because she said I could tell you . But *only* you. And she sent me this." Frau Molnar fumbled in her handbag and brought out a mobile: not a fancy smartphone, just a basic model.

"There was a note inside the package it came in," explained Frau Molnar. "Telling me the phone is brand new, no previous owner. The only number in its memory is that of another new mobile – which is hers. A secure link. She'd like you to give her a call."

I accepted the phone, saying: "This is not the place. I'll do it later."

There seemed to be no more information to be squeezed out of Frau Molnar, so we spent the rest of the evening chatting about less painful subjects.

Thirty-Seven

After dinner, in the privacy of my room at Donaublick, I fired up my new mobile and rang the only number. It was answered almost immediately by a familiar voice: Josie's.

"So you *have* been to see Frau Molnar!"

I replied: "She's told me everything. Quite a story. What do you want me to do?"

"Now that Werner may know Feldmann is dead, I have to be doubly careful. We need to talk, but not over the phone. Can you come to Berlin?"

"Berlin! I must be nearly a thousand kilometres away."

"In your racing car, only two days. Please!"

"When do you want to see me?"

"The sooner the better. Did you see that date in the diary I left in the car?"

"The 30th September. We've been puzzling over it ever since. What's its significance?"

"I don't know exactly. That's the problem. I'm sure Werner has *something* planned for that day and I have all sorts of theories. Too many theories. I need another brain on the job. Tomorrow is the 26th, so we're running out of time."

"Two days should be no problem, but why Berlin?"

"I needed to find somewhere safe. Well away from Werner and anything to do with the DDR. I'm staying with an old friend no one else knows about. Happens to be in Berlin."

"Okay, where do we meet?"

"Berlin is a big city with the usual car problems, so why not dump your car at the Lindtner and take a train from there. The weather forecast is good, temperature warm for the time of year, and I know just the place where we can sit out. When you arrive in Berlin, hop on the U-Bahn to Stadtmitte, from where it's a one-minute walk to Gendarmenmarkt. On the corner of Jägerstrasse, facing the concert house, is a restaurant. Not expensive, ideal for people watching. And trying to crack the riddle of Werner Breitling. Meet me the day after tomorrow at seven in the evening. That should give us three days until zero hour, when whatever Werner is hatching is due to happen."

I promised to be there.

Thirty-Eight

Berlin's Gendarmenmarkt is a neoclassical masterpiece, one of the world's great city sights. I'd been there briefly during my futile attempt to drum up business in that other DDR, the German Democratic Republic, when the square had been a showpiece for Communist sloth and incompetence. Although the concert house had been in fairly good shape, the two flanking churches were still shells. Forty years after the Red Army had rolled in, almost nothing had been done except clear up wartime rubble.

After reunification the go-getters of West Germany had quickly brought the square back to its former glory – perhaps even better. When I arrived, Josie was already there, sitting at a table facing a spectacular floodlit scene.

When I say Josie was sitting there, I almost took the next table, assuming she had yet to arrive, because Frau Chameleon had engineered another transformation. I had seen red hair and blue hair; now it was the turn of black – probably its natural colour. If you are in hiding, you don't want to stand out like a beacon. She could almost have walked into party headquarters in Dresden without anyone recognising her.

I gave her a hug and – was it my imagination? – had she put on weight? Maybe her escape from extreme politics had made for a clearer conscience and better health.

When we had ordered and drinks were on the table, I said: "There's a lot I don't know, so start at the beginning."

Josie thought for a moment.

"I met Jonny, my first boyfriend, while still in my teens. I thought he could do no wrong and when he started the German Democratic Right I was swept away by the glamour. It was all so *exciting*. Those early days were the best, that's for sure.

"When Jonny left home, it was an awful shock. Had it been for another woman, I might have understood, but no – he was almost a puritan in that respect – it was for a *different* sort of love, his political party.

"By this time I was doing most of the office work and had Karl to look after, so no time to feel sorry for myself. Had to soldier on. But at the back of my mind… I was beginning…"

"To doubt?" I suggested.

"I wouldn't admit it, even to myself. Jonny was so charismatic, so *persuasive*, you believed all he told you."

I asked: "When did Werner come into your life?"

"Gradually. He joined the party early on. Exactly when I'm not too sure, because he creeps up on you. Although a big man, he doesn't usually throw his weight around. He… he *slinks*."

"But you…" I hunted for tactful words. "…You made Werner welcome in your house."

She shrugged. "Jonny had left. I was alone. It suited both of us."

"But Jonny's death changed everything?" I suggested.

She nodded. "For a while I was… like, drugged. Wandered around in a daze. Didn't wake up until after the funeral."

"When you found Werner Breitling was now the party's… not its 'Führer', but its 'Leiter'."

She smiled at the distinction and continued: "Now things changed fast. At least, in my head. Unlike Jonny, Werner doesn't even *try* to persuade. He recites the party line and you toe it."

"Those that don't…?" I made a slitting motion across my throat.

She nodded. "I found I was being sidelined. Werner was happy for me to continue with the donkey work, but now that's all I was: the DDR's donkey. And I noticed for the first time that Sepp Feldmann was Werner's lapdog. On the odd occasions I went up to the office I'd catch them whispering in corners; plotting, but keeping the rest of us in the dark."

"Feldmann, a man with a criminal record," I said.

"Which I only discovered when I started having my doubts and did some digging."

"You began to wonder if Feldmann had killed Jonny?"

She nodded. "Once that possibility hit me, I couldn't let it go. Feldmann had been on the Kurort Rathen with Jonny. It couldn't have been a coincidence."

"A frightening thought."

"Terrifying. Once born, thoughts don't go away. If Werner and Sepp had ganged up to kill Jonny, I could be next. As long as I behaved myself I should be safe, because the police would start taking an interest if DDR members started dying in serious numbers. But if I stepped out of line, became a threat, they might become desperate."

"But you were brave enough – foolhardy, really – to meet Feldmann alone when he came to see you in Visegrad."

"By then I'd become angry. And *very* curious. When Werner virtually ordered me to take a holiday, I suspected he wanted me out of the way."

"He gave you a mission," I said. "To check out Hungary's migrant border. Was that a smokescreen?"

"Pretty much," she replied. "No doubt he was interested, but I think the real reason he sent me off to Hungary was to get me off the premises. In any organisation there are bound to be leaks. That mysterious word 'Königstein' had made its appearance, with no agenda attached but obviously important."

"I thought you were being careful to keep Werner in the dark about your movements, yet he knew you would be spending two days with Frau Molnar on the way back."

Josie looked shamefaced. "It was driving me *crazy*. Was I being paranoid? Or was Werner really planning to get rid of me? I *had to* know. So when I sent off my report about our meeting with Frank in Mohacs, I mentioned that I'd be stopping off in Visegrad on the way back."

"Offering yourself as bait," I said.

She nodded. "Being a long way from home might be an incentive for him to try something. The Hungarians would know nothing of our background; might treat any incident as simply some crazy foreigners settling a score on their soil."

"Even so, it must have been quite a shock when Werner took the bait and Feldmann turned up on Frau Molnar's doorstep."

"You can say that again. I'd made no plans for this actually happening. Sepp arrived with some story about important party matters to discuss, so I put him off. Said I'd not had dinner, suggested we meet in a couple of hours in the centre of town by the church. He agreed and went off."

"Then you *did* make some plans?"

She nodded. "Jonny had been killed with a knife, so Sepp would probably try the same with me. Guns are difficult to get hold of and noisy; physical assaults can go wrong and may also end up noisy. So I bet my life on a knife and chose my own weapon, the nastiest one I could find in Frau Molnar's kitchen."

"A duel to the death with knives," I mused. "Against a man who had probably already killed. You must have been nuts."

Josie nodded. "Which is why I took my old buddy Attila along. Dogs are pack animals, always ready to protect their masters. A knife *and* a Rottweiler should tip the balance in my favour."

"And it worked. When Feldmann attacked, Attila came to the rescue."

Josie grimaced. "It didn't happen in quite the way I told Frau Molnar. There was no 'grabbing me round the neck', which might have given me a sporting chance. No, Sepp already had his knife out, ready to strike before I became aware of him. It was dark, so he must have assumed I was alone. But Attila had a sharper ear, better senses, and tore his lead from my hand. Before I knew what was going on, he was behind me, at Feldmann's throat. I couldn't have stopped him even if I'd wanted to. He went berserk. But Sepp already had his knife out and used it to fight off Attila."

"So Feldmann killed Attila!" I said. Molnar hadn't known how her dog had died, but now the drama was starting to make sense.

"Even a Rottweiler doesn't stand much of a chance against a knife," said Josie. "But he put up a terrific fight. Made a horrible mess of Sepp."

"And *you* finished Feldmann off?"

Josie sat silent for a moment, as she remembered. Then said: "I still can't believe what I did. In front of me, covered in blood but still alive, was the man who'd killed my Jonny. Like Attila, I went crazy. Stabbed and stabbed."

"And then went back to tell Frau Molnar?"

Josie nodded. "Eventually. First I just sat there, on the ground, two bloody corpses in front of me. Forced myself not to panic. To think it through. I'd killed a man, which was a crime. But I could claim self-defence, so my first instinct was to hand myself in. Then I thought again. Why was I in this mess? Because Werner was hunting me down, apparently prepared to do anything to stop me. Stop me doing what? It could only be that Jonny, our party's old guard, and I were getting in the way of Breitling's new order. Was 30th September part of this new order? Whatever it was, I was now the only one who could stop him. And I could not do that from a police cell."

Josie gave a little shiver, took a sip of wine.

I said. "When you returned to Donaublick, you told Frau Molnar that Attila had killed Feldmann. Said nothing about knives. Why?"

"To remain free, I needed help. Molnar was my only candidate. The bodies were lying only metres from a main road and would be discovered within hours of daybreak. If I did nothing, Molnar would then identify her dog, instantly make the connection, and by lunchtime my face would appear under a 'Wanted' notice in every European police station. I needed to delay discovery of the bodies, which meant getting Molnar on my side. The only way I could do that was to spin her the story that her dog had killed my assailant. Like me, she would then be keen to cover it all up."

"What did you do with the knives?"

"Carefully cleaned them and returned Molnar's to its original place. Sepp's I threw far into the Danube, where it sank without trace."

"You seem to have thought of everything," I said, trying to absorb what Josie had just told me.

Berlin still retained much summer warmth, while in front of us the Gendarmenmarkt sparkled under countless lights. But I was hardly aware of our setting. We sat there silently for some moments, each with our own thoughts. Then I remembered Karl, the little lad who seemed to have no qualms about his missing mother. So I said:

"When I picked up Karl, he was amazingly calm. As if he knew you were okay. Did he?"

She smiled. "If I had to disappear for a while, I couldn't leave the poor boy in limbo. So I arranged for you to pick him up…"

"…Crafty girl!"

"…And gave him a special phone, same as you. We manage a short text chat most evenings. I told him this had to be a secret; between the two of us. Karl is good at keeping secrets."

"He sure is. Hasn't even told me."

Do you think I've done the right thing?" she asked, suddenly shy.

"Right thing with Karl?"

"No, no. I mean killing Sepp… not going to the police… disappearing… everything."

"I think you've been very *brave*," I replied, diplomatically. "And you're still free. Has it been worth it? I don't know. You don't seem to have discovered much, except that something *might* happen on the 30th September."

"I'd hoped to do better," she admitted. "Especially as Sepp's smartphone was in his pocket and I was able to take it over. I spent hours going through the messages, to get a feel for his style, which was always brief, giving nothing away. In the end, I tapped out just two words: 'Job done'. Sent it off to Werner."

"Pretending to be Feldmann?"

She nodded. "After we'd buried the bodies, I made my way to Berlin, settled in with my friend, and continued impersonating Sepp. Not too difficult, as he would also be lying low."

"But Werner has revealed nothing?"

186

"He's a canny operator, very security conscious, but I wouldn't say I've learnt *nothing*. One of the messages already on the phone I inherited was 'Ahmed has agreed'."

"'Ahmed'. Sounds Islamic."

"Perhaps. Anyway, *not* the sort of person I'd expect the leader of the DDR to have anything to do with."

"'Germany for Germans', I believe is your motto."

Josie nodded. "A couple of days after I arrived in Berlin, there was another message: 'Ahmed in place'. I didn't know what this meant – still don't – but Sepp probably did, so I just replied: 'Well done with Ahmed'."

"Werner was not suspicious?"

"At this stage, I don't think so. Because almost immediately a message came back: 'Can you return soon?' To which I replied: 'Job more difficult than anticipated: will return when able'."

"What did Werner say to that?"

"Nothing. But Sepp was Werner's hit-man, so the fact that he was wanted back suggests…?"

"That Feldmann is in line for that job on the 30th?"

Josie nodded. "*We* know Sepp will not be returning, so if Werner wants anything done, he'll now have to fix it himself."

"No other potential assassins lurking in the corridors of your offices?" A nasty jibe, but I couldn't resist it.

Josie took it well. Replied: "Even in the DDR, killers don't grow on trees."

Thirty-Nine

We finished our meal in subdued mood. Josie said she would stay in Berlin, monitoring any more messages that might come in. If the Hungarian police stayed with their theory that the body in the wood was a German gangland killing, worth little effort or publicity, Werner might continue to believe Josef Feldmann was still at large. If he suspected the truth, she would be safely incognito in the big city.

We parted just after 9.30 – Josie to her undisclosed hiding place, me to a pre-booked room at the nearby Hilton. I phoned Fischer, but on this occasion it was so late I could only leave a message and extract a promise he would call back in the morning. I bought a double Laphroaig at the bar for a stupid price and sat down to sift through the evidence; see if I could come to any conclusion. I got nowhere and eventually drifted off to bed, where I slept badly.

Next morning Chief Inspector Fischer, the man who

was open nearly all hours, phoned while I was still shaving. Time for some multi-tasking, so I continued shaving with my right hand while I recounted the events of the previous evening into a phone held in my left. However, I nicked my chin, leaving the Hilton's nice white towels spotted with blood, so had to bring task one to a premature conclusion and concentrate on task two. When I'd finished my side of it, Fischer said:

"Thanks to our monitoring team, we knew about the 'Ahmed' exchanges between Breitling and – supposedly – Feldmann. These surprised us as well, because the DDR leader would not normally be seen near anyone with a name like Ahmed. We were even more surprised when one of our surveillance guys managed to get a photo of the two of them together, apparently the best of pals."

"You're sure it was Ahmed?"

"We ran the name and photo through our computers and confirmation came within minutes. The man Breitling had been chatting to was Ahmed Aziz, thirty-three years old, originally from Mosul in Iraq."

"Surely not a Jihadi?"

"Most unlikely. Aziz has never appeared on our radar and ticks none of the bad boxes. We only know he found life impossible in Mosul, so fled to Syria, which turned out to be from the frying pan into the fire. He managed to get out of Syria as well, finished up four years ago here in Germany. Speaks fluent English, now pretty good in German. Claims to be an engineer, although in view of his background can't have had much practical experience; in Iraq and Syria things tend to be knocked down rather than put up."

"Does he have a job?"

"He works for Dresden Council, emptying refuse bins."

"What on earth does he have in common with Breitling?"

Fischer sighed. "If only we knew. People who come to our attention usually have some question marks against them, but Aziz seems to be a migrant whose sole aim is to improve himself; has applied for German citizenship and is on course to get it."

"So where does this leave us?" I asked.

"Frustrated," replied Fischer. "We can only wait and see."

"While keeping a watchful eye on Breitling and Aziz?"

"Of course. It's now the 28th, only two days to go. If we receive no further information, I'll send all available resources to Königstein on the 30th. Not that I think they'll do much good; I have a nasty feeling we're missing something, but can't afford to ignore such an obvious pointer."

"What do you want me to do?"

"Return to the good Frau Lindtner. Await developments. And keep close to your mobile."

Forty

I was back in the Hotel Lindtner by early afternoon, in time for the evening rush. Trudi welcomed me with even more enthusiasm than usual, which I put down to her having missed my Casanova charms. However, it turned out to be more because there was a convention of horologists in town and it was all hands to the pumps for the hotel staff. I hardly stopped for five hours, which had the merit of taking my mind off other things.

It must have been close to midnight by the time our horologists called time on time, as it were, and Trudi was able to lock that dining room door, get out the Jägermeister and listen to my latest sitrep.

When I'd finished, she asked: "What happens now?"

"We wait,"

"For what?"

"The 30th. Day after tomorrow."

"Just a date in a diary. Probably a wild goose chase."

"A date based on information coming out of DDR headquarters."

"Information!" Trudi was dismissive. "Nothing more than guesswork."

"Maybe. But Fischer and his team have a lot of experience in reading the runes. Of course they'll be wrong much of the time, but all non-events are a triumph. What he *can't* afford is for the terrorist to score even a single goal. Fischer's is a no-win situation: succeed and nobody is aware of it, so he gets no thanks; fail just once and the roof falls in, there are questions in the Bundestag and his career goes down the tube."

Trudi nodded, accepting my point, and asked: "I imagine you'll want the day off on the 30th? Just in case."

"If you don't mind."

"Will you be joining Fischer's troops in Königstein?"

"I think not. Fischer made a comment about feeling he was missing something. I feel I'm missing something about Josie. She's just survived an attempt on her life, then killed her attacker. Enough to turn most girls into gibbering wrecks. Yet the Josie I met yesterday had, I swear, put on weight…"

"Not difficult for someone starting at starvation level. Any change has to be up."

"And she seems to have… somehow matured. Is now more content, knows where she's going."

"You're imagining things. Anyway, you said Josie would be staying in Berlin. Isn't… whatever it is… supposed to be happening around here?"

I nodded. "So this is where I'll hang around. For want of anything better."

Then, for no apparent reason, I remembered Josie had a son. So asked: "How's Karl doing?"

192

"I feed him, send him to school, where he says he has plenty of friends; put him to bed. A model guest. Seems happy enough."

"Karl would understand when say I shall start the big day on the bench: in reserve," I said. If anything *does* happen I can then respond to the call: swing into action. And, if I'm really fantasising, score the deciding goal."

"You *are* fantasising," said Trudi. "You're delirious. Nothing will happen. You look awful. Whacked. Come on, time for bed."

I didn't object. And under her soothing treatment slept like a king.

Forty-One

The 30th September dawned blustery and cooler, with intermittent sun; distinctly autumnal. I got Karl off to school, telling him I'd just met his mother and she sent her love. His secret need be a secret no longer – at least not from me. He smiled, said he was good at keeping secrets, and trotted off happily. With his parental history – father murdered, mother a killer and fugitive – psychologists would no doubt forecast dire results for the lad, but most children seem to be tough little beasts, rolling with the punches that early life throws at them.

I had a brief call from Chief Inspector Fischer, to make sure I was ready if needed and telling me most of his team were now policing Königstein. I then spent much of the morning mooching around the hotel, unable to settle. Waiting… for what?

Just after 12.30 my mobile rang. It was Josie.

"Where are you…?" I began

She cut me short: "Never mind about that. Have you read the latest *Dresdner Rundschau*?"

I had not. But most hotels in Germany keep a selection of national and local newspapers in their restaurant for customers to browse through, so I replied that I could. But why? What was I looking for?

"Read it and see if anything strikes you," she replied. "When you've found it, ring back. But tell no one."

"Not even the Chief Inspector?"

"*Especially* not Fischer."

I was about to protest, but had been cut off. I didn't like the sound of this, but first had to work out what she was on about. I went to the dining room, which was about to open for lunch, and found the *Dresdner Rundschau* hanging in its wooden spine on the newspaper rack. Sat down and started going through it. Item by item.

Helge Schmidt had given birth to triplets; Wilhelm Braun had died aged 105; the Saxon Assembly had approved a transgender motion. Hardly gripping stuff.

So when I saw the headline 'Saxon Steamship's Maiden Voyage', my experience on the Kurort Rathen triggered a mild interest. I read that their new paddle steamer, number ten and last of the line, which should have been ready at the start of the summer season, would now be accepting its first paying guests. On the 30th September the Königstein would set sail from Dresden quay at 2pm, with a host of dignitaries, for a champagne inaugural trip...

I broke into a cold sweat. Königstein... 30th September. That was today! Now! To be precise, in a little over one hour. Chief Inspector Fischer had, as feared, missed something. We all had. Königstein did not refer to the castle or the town, but a boat; one that was only joining the fleet today, so no one had made the connection. Fischer's troops would be swarming all over Königstein the place, while I was stranded almost as far from the action. No hope that either of us could reach Dresden Quay in time for Königstein the boat's departure.

But that ought not to be necessary. There were such things as phones. Fischer only had to ring his office and he could have men at the scene within minutes: plenty of time to check out the steamer and, if necessary, abort the sailing.

But Josie had said not to tell Fischer. Had been most insistent. What was she playing at? Who should I trust? A painted hippy who had run a far-right party, then killed a man? Or a top cop? On the face of it, a no-brainer, but I hesitated. I felt I now knew the painted hippy rather well. Instinct told me her politics were no longer extreme; she seemed confident, in control of the situation – whatever that 'situation' might be.

In search of guidance to resolve my dilemma, I returned to the *Rundschau* article.

In common with her nine sisters in the fleet, the Königstein had been a veteran rescued from a knacker's yard. Lots of love and cash had then been lavished on her to produce a vessel that was as close to its 19th-century original as efficient operating and modern safety standards would allow. This had nearly broken the bank – several times – and had taken much longer than anticipated; this first sailing had been delayed three times during the course of the summer.

The Königstein had finally passed all her tests and, under the command of Captain Ansbacher, was ready for her maiden voyage; a short celebratory procession upstream towards Pirna and back, about three hours in all. To underline the Saxon State's commitment to racial harmony and integration, the company was delighted to announce that Königstein's second engineer was to be the very experienced Ahmed Aziz, originally from Iraq.

For a moment I sat there, paralysed. This was the Ahmed of cryptic emails between Breitling and Feldmann; Ahmed the migrant, seen chatting amicably to the DDR leader, whose public ethos was hatred of migrants. A man who hailed from a country that was a prime exporter of violence, yet had been assessed by Fischer, who should know, as no threat. What was I supposed to believe?

My brain a jumble, I rang Josie, who answered at once.

"Interesting, eh?" was her opening comment.

"No good sitting on our backsides, saying 'interesting'," I snapped, then insisted: "We need to tell Fischer. Pretty damned quick."

"Fischer will hear in good time. But not yet."

"I hope you know what you're doing." I was exasperated beyond belief. "The Königstein sailing must have been in Breitling's sights for weeks. His tame Iraqi is now in place…"

"…Tame Iraqi?" Josie interrupted. "Werner *loathes* foreigners."

"Well, yes…" In my brain, confusion reigned supreme. "…But they're behaving like old pals."

"Werner can be a slimy bastard."

"You mean…?"

"I mean you should fire up your silver racer and get yourself to the Elbe quay in Dresden. To see the show."

I was appalled. "There'll be hundreds of people on that boat, including women and children. All innocent. Whose side are you on?"

"Come on, Ed! Werner killed my Jonny. Tried to do the same to me. How can you even *begin* to think I'd still be working for him?"

"I know, but… What the hell *is* going on?"

"It's called retribution… No, it's more than that. I want to come out of hiding. Return to the world. Which means ridding myself of that… that awful thing…"

"You mean Werner?"

"Just get yourself to Dresden. I need you there for support. Don't worry, there'll be no big bang: at least not while all those people are on board. Trust me."

"You're *crazy*. We *must* tell Fischer."

"*I* will tell Fischer. But only when the time is right." She repeated: "Trust me."

Although there was no one to see me, I shook my head in disbelief. For better or worse, I *would* trust Josie. Was I also totally mad?

"You win," I said. "I'm on my way."

Forty-Two

On my way to where? By the time I reached Königstein's moorings she would have left, but this was billed as a tour of three hours in the direction of Pirna. Which was in *my* direction. I should be able to intercept it.

With destination unknown, Satnav would not be much use, so I went back to basics – an atlas – which showed a road running conveniently east, then south, along the bank of the Elbe. If I approached Dresden along that, Königstein and I should meet up. After rushing around to find Trudi and giving her a frantic account of what was happening, I leapt into my Porsche and headed north.

By the time I reached the suburb of Blasewitz, I was becoming concerned, because the river, which had to be somewhere on my right, remained hidden by buildings. Then, without warning, buildings gave way to fields. But no river. The Elbe flood plain was so wide here that the river was some distance away and hidden from view. For a minute or two I continued driving, trying to see if I could spot any distant funnels, while at the same time avoiding crashing my Porsche. But the river remained obscured. By now I was getting so close to Dresden centre, I could have passed the steamer without seeing her, so I did an about turn at the next intersection and headed back, intent on finding a riverside spot they could not yet have reached.

I was in luck. Turning left at the first major junction, I found myself approaching what looked like London's Albert Bridge over the Thames. A sign caught my eye, which took me down to a car park on the river's bank, almost under what was indeed a bridge. I parked the Porsche.

I later learnt that this latticed Victorian confection was the Loschwitz Bridge, otherwise known as the Blue Wonder. At the time I was less interested in architectural treasures than getting myself to a river viewpoint, so I sprinted up to the footpath over the Blue Wonder, hoping I was in time.

I was. Well, I was in time to see a paddle steamer, about three hundred yards downstream, making slow progress against the current in my direction. It was bows on, so I couldn't see the name, but an Oompah band was making festive sounds on the upper deck, so it *had* to be the Königstein.

Whether I was in time for our forecast catastrophe was an entirely different matter. There was absolutely nothing I could do, standing there on the Blue Wonder bridge. But looking down on this ordinary scene, in peaceful, well-regulated Deutschland, it was temping to think I'd simply been caught up in a web of hysteria. Then I remembered my own experience, stumbling across the body of Jonny Kästner in the Kurort Rathen's engine room. That had been real enough. And unless Fischer and Josie were combining in a macabre joke, Feldmann and Attila really *had* been buried in a Hungarian forest.

No sooner had I convinced myself we faced some sort of disaster, than my addled brain seesawed to a contrary argument: if this was the Königstein, why was it still afloat and obviously doing very well? It was now nearly quarter to three, so it must have been under way for at least half an hour. Any mischief should surely have manifested itself by now.

I watched as the boat passed directly beneath me and continued upstream towards Pirna. An awning covered the upper deck so I couldn't see the band, but there was a crescendo of jollity as it passed. Meanwhile, the open lower decks slipped past in an alcoholic paradise of champagne glasses.

As these sounds receded, another caught my attention. Again coming from the direction of Dresden. This time not human generated but mechanical: the rhythmic thump of helicopter blades.

It was flying fast for a chopper and within seconds was over the bridge. The logo read 'Polizei'. It made straight for the boat. They were close enough for me to hear the message it kept blasting out:

"Everyone disembark immediately. I say again, find the nearest mooring and disembark immediately."

'Sofort', the German for 'at once', was delivered so often and so loudly there was no room for any misunderstanding. Even so, Königstein continued upstream for at least another minute before anything seemed to happen. Then, very slowly, the speed and noise dropped off. For a moment the boat wallowed in the Elbe, before starting to drift back with the current.

My viewpoint on the bridge had served its purpose. Exactly where the Königstein would land was uncertain, but I now needed to be at river level, so sprinted back to the car park where I'd left my Porsche. As I got there, the chopper came to rest on a vacant patch at the far end. Two figures emerged, bending low to avoid the rotor blades. Both were wearing protective bullet-proof 'Polizei' vests. One of them was Chief Inspector Helmut Fischer.

Under the direction of the helicopter and two men on the ground, the Königstein was reversing with the current towards where we were standing, the plan clearly to moor up beside the car park; although not a recognised quay, it should prove easy enough to get everyone off the boat.

As the steamer edged towards land, screaming sirens and flashing lights announced the arrival of reinforcements. By the time the first mooring lines were being thrown from the boat, Fischer had a dozen men ready for action.

The name gleaming on the paddle housing was indeed the Königstein. As she came to rest against the bank, it became clear that getting people off would not, after all, be that easy, because paddles protrude, so the boat could not be brought alongside in the usual way. On board someone was preparing the gangplank, but Fischer was having none of it: disembarking a load of semi-sozzled partygoers down such a narrow exit would take far too long. He ordered the bow to be made fast, then told the captain to put the helm hard to starboard and give her a short burst of power. This brought the stern out into the river and the front half hard up against the bank, where the police stood ready to help people off.

Transport vehicles that fly have to prove they can evacuate everyone within 90 seconds – a tall order with perhaps 400 souls on board. I've no idea what the rules are for *floating* public transport vehicles, but Fischer was having the problem that always occurs in real emergencies: passengers trying to leave with all their possessions. Some were reluctant to abandon glasses that still contained champagne; most of the ladies would not be parted from their handbags; one rouged and wrinkled old dear was insisting that her obese Dachshund was far too precious to be left behind.

The operation was further slowed by the possibility of wet feet. Although the Königstein lay low in the water, with only a short jump into the helping hands of safety, many passengers dithered on the brink. Fischer became increasingly impatient, yelling at everyone to hurry it along.

Finally, the job was done. The captain, a trim man in his fifties with a neat, greying beard, was the last to leave, saying he had personally checked that no one remained on board.

Everyone relaxed. The Chief Inspector managed a weary smile. What now? Had this panic really been necessary? No hostages had been taken; no shots fired; the paddle steamer was lying there, unthreatening.

It was probably because everyone was focussed on the river that we didn't at first notice a rumpus behind us. There was a scuffle, then a figure emerged, ran to the bow of the Königstein and hauled himself on board; onto the vessel that had just been evacuated because of a terrorist scare.

It wasn't until he started running aft and came into profile that I saw who it was: Werner Breitling.

Chief Inspector Fischer hesitated. The boat had been cleared, his job done. The Königstein would lie there, quarantined, until the arrival of the explosives experts. It would be reckless to order any of his officers on board while there remained the slightest risk of an explosion. On the other hand, why was the notorious DDR leader defying a police cordon to leap onto what could be a lethal boat? Only one rational answer: he wanted to remove incriminating evidence. If the law was to stand any chance of securing a conviction, that evidence must remain intact.

Fischer started an intense discussion with one of his men. You didn't need to be a genius to work out what it was about: should he send someone to bring Breitling off the boat?

For my part, the jigsaw was starting to have some meaning. Although pieces were still missing, the final picture was beginning to emerge.

So far I'd been just a figure in the crowd. Fischer had been busy and not seen me. But now I needed to speak to him. At the top of my voice, I yelled: "Helmut!"

Hearing his given name in a work environment did the trick. Startled, he looked up. Saw me. Broke off the conversation with his colleague and strode over.

"What the hell are *you* doing here?"

"Josie sent me."

"Where is she?"

"Don't know." This was an honest answer, although I suspected she was no longer in Berlin. I added: "She was worried about the Königstein. Asked me to drive up and keep an eye on it."

"You've done that and I'm busy…" Fischer started to move off.

"Stop!" I said urgently. "Don't send any of your men onto that boat."

He turned round. "What do you mean?"

My reply was another question: "Where's Ahmed Aziz?"

"I assume he's safely ashore with the rest of them. The captain reported the ship clear."

"Then don't risk any of your men. There could still be some device hidden away. Wait for your bomb disposal team."

"Breitling could be up to all sorts of things…"

"Let him. It's not worth risking any of your men."

"Is there something you're not telling me?"

I shook my head. "Just guessing."

I could see Fischer did not believe me. But my plea had hit a nerve. He realised I was right. If the Königstein exploded with one of his officers onboard his career would lie in ruins.

"Might be an idea to get everyone further back," I suggested. "Just in case."

Fischer gave me a glare for telling him how to do his job, but again knew I was right. Told his men to move the crowd away from the river.

The sensation caused by that mysterious figure scrambling to board the forbidden vessel soon subsided. The passengers – and now a few onlookers – followed police orders and began ambling further into the car park. A few started making their way up the slope towards the town.

Like many of us, I had my back to the river when it happened. There wasn't much noise, more a muffled roar. But the ground shook.

I turned to see a cloud of debris swirling over the Königstein. Then a lick of flame, which gradually took hold. The chatter stopped as people enjoyed – if that was the right word – this unexpected conclusion to their river trip; after the champagne party, the fireworks. Guy Fawkes on the Elbe, although few Germans would have heard about this very British festival.

Chief Inspector Fischer, like the rest of us, stood there mesmerised. No doubt hardly believing his luck. Mission accomplished, with no casualties for the good guys. But with the enemy leader being satisfactorily incinerated before his eyes.

Forty-Three

Dresden and the Upper Elbe made the most of its moment in the limelight. It's not often in this vale of tears that virtue is rewarded, wickedness pays the price and we live happily ever after. The world's media, from Aalborg to Zimbabwe, from Aitutaki to Zagreb, celebrated the triumph of good over evil.

A few misguided souls sought to make a hero of Werner Breitling, a man of principle they said, even if you did not agree with him; someone who died doing what he thought was right. No one could explain *what* he was doing on the Königstein; or why whatever he was doing might be right.

The death of the paddle steamer was riddled with unanswered questions. For starters: *Who* had planted the bomb? *Why* had they done it? *How* had the plot been uncovered?

As one of those most intimately involved, I wanted to find the answers. I had plenty of theories, but had been wrong so often in the past I sometimes doubted my own sanity. I needed… what everyone seems to need these days: closure.

My gateway to possible closure came the next day when discussing the event with Trudi, who was agog for the inside story. She mentioned that Karl would not be returning to us after school tonight because his mother was back at home.

Karl's mother: Josie Kästner. Just the person to unlock that treasure chest of truths. I left it until late afternoon, when Karl and therefore Josie should be at home. My call was answered on the second ring.

"Did you enjoy the show?" Frau Kästner sounded in good spirits.

"How did you know?" I asked.

"I didn't *know*. But obviously *something* could happen."

"It wasn't at all obvious. Not to me."

"Maybe I owe you an explanation."

"No 'maybe' about it."

"Coffee tomorrow at eleven, then? Usual place."

"Gendarmenmarkt, Berlin?"

She giggled. "You know where I mean."

"I've given up trying to work out *what* you mean and *where* you mean," I grumbled.

"Come by yourself," she said.

"No Trudi?"

"Best we keep it to the three of us."

"Three? Karl knows?"

"Karl knows almost nothing."

"So who else?"

"Tomorrow at eleven."

The phone went dead.

Forty-Four

Next day I mounted my silver Porsche and rode her up the familiar hairpins to the Kästner residence. The blue Dacia, wing mirror still dangling, was parked outside; just like old times. But what was that? Another car, a black Toyota. Herr Breitling's, if I was not mistaken. The man everyone said had departed to the nether regions.

It was with a slightly queasy feeling that I knocked on the door. It was opened by a Frau Kästner, who I swear had put on weight. She would still have been on the light side of 50 kilos, so hardly obese, but she was now some way from skeletal. Her lip adornment was also absent so all that remained from the old Josie were the tattoos, which were less easy to remove. She looked in fine fettle, as though an exciting life suited her.

She gave me an extra big hug, invited me in and said: "There's someone I'd like you to meet."

Since the fireworks display on the Elbe, more pieces of the jigsaw had slotted into place, so I wasn't entirely surprised. The man in front of me was of medium height, with a lightly tanned complexion and small moustache, about the same age as Josie. Fischer had said he spoke good English, so I greeted him in that language:

"Mr. Ahmed Aziz, late of Mosul, I believe."

He shook my hand, smiled and said, also in English: "Via a few other places."

"From where they export trouble, which you seem to have brought with you." I had meant to sound sympathetic, but realised my comment could be taken two ways, so added: "Not your fault, of course."

"Come on, you two. Coffee's ready." Josie led the way into her parlour. We followed. Sat down.

Returning to German, Josie said: "For reasons that'll become clear, what's said here must remain between the three of us."

"No Trudi?"

"No anyone."

"Chief Inspector Fischer is no fool; he'll have guessed most of it."

"Let him guess. As long as we remain schtum, he won't be able to *prove* anything ."

"I seem to have been the one who started it all," I said. "When I found the body of poor Jonny. But Josie, you said it wasn't until after the funeral you began to suspect Werner. When do you think he realised you were on to him?"

"Probably a gradual process. Jonny's death had shaken us all and it took a while for things to settle down. At first I didn't realise how ambitious Werner was; or what he was after. But when he and Sepp started muttering about organising something that would *really* focus attention on the party, I began to worry. The DDR had always been politically way-out, but Jonny had been careful to play things by the book. It began to dawn on me that Werner didn't see it the same way."

"He sent you off to Hungary to get rid of you?"

She nodded. "So he and Sepp could go about their planning without any prying eyes or ears. He couldn't afford another assassination so soon after getting rid of Jonny. But when I rang from Mohacs to tell him I would be stopping off in Visegrad, he saw his chance of a more permanent solution with little apparent risk. So Sepp was sent off to do the dirty."

"With the result we all know," I said. "Including Chief Inspector Fischer, who told me he was pretty sure you must have killed Feldmann."

"Fischer can think what he likes," said Josie. "The only murder weapon found at the scene was poor faithful Attila. To whom I owe my life."

"The autopsy showed Attila did not kill Feldmann," I pointed out. "He died from multiple knife wounds."

"A foreign career criminal is found savaged by a Rottweiler with injuries that could have proved fatal. Is any police force going to squander valuable time and money trying to prove otherwise?"

"I hope you're right," I said.

"But it's one reason to keep this as our secret," she conceded.

"*One* reason? Is there another?"

Josie thought for a moment, then said: "Ahmed should tell you what happened next." She pronounced his name with the throaty 'H', Arab style.

"You'll have heard about my background from Fischer," he began. He spoke German with quite an accent, not as well as English. "I've been here four years, doing whatever jobs I can pick up. In Iraq I was an engineer, but here migrants usually have to settle for more menial work. So I empty dustbins. It's the price we pay for freedom and a safer environment. But there's a lot of anti-migrant feeling, so the government is trying to do something about it; by getting us out of our migrant ghettos and into jobs. They knew I was an engineer, but even so I was amazed when the Saxon Steamship offer came up from – of all people – Herr Breitling."

"Amazed because he was the leader of the DDR?"

Ahmed nodded. "The man who made a habit of bad-mouthing us was offering me a job. It didn't make sense."

"Breitling didn't work for the Steamship company," I said. "So how *could he* offer you that job?"

"Feldmann *did* work for the company," Josie pointed out. "Remember?"

I remembered only too well.

"We assume Sepp went to Werner," continued Josie. "Told him about the vacancy – a migrant preferred – and Werner just brokered the deal."

"All I know is that this man Breitling, whom I'd heard of but never met, came to me out of the blue," said Ahmed. "Said if I applied for the Steamship job I'd probably get it. I couldn't understand it, but had nothing to lose, so I applied."

"And got it," I said. "Better than emptying dustbins."

Josie said: "Werner was keeping me in the dark about everything, so I only got to hear about this when Feldmann died and I took over his phone. Like Ahmed, I couldn't understand what was going on, but by now I was suspicious about everything Werner was up to and had to find out. It was tricky, because I was holed up in Berlin and scared of going anywhere near Dresden, but eventually I found a friend who was able to pass on a message: if Ahmed could meet me in Berlin, I would pay his train fare and he would learn something to his advantage."

"Ahmed smiled: "That train journey saved my life."

"And the lives of everyone on the Königstein," said Josie. "Fortunately, Ahmed and I hit it off at once. I don't know why, but we trusted each other."

"I was also becoming suspicious," said Ahmed. "After that strange first meeting with Breitling, I didn't see him again for a while. My buddy was Sepp Feldmann, because he also worked for the company. He probably made a special effort to be nice, so we got on pretty well. Then Sepp vanished. No one seemed to know why or where. Instead, Breitling returned. Didn't like him at all. I think he also tried to be friendly, but it didn't work…"

"Werner didn't do 'friendly'," said Josie.

"He was nervous, jumpy, forever asking if I was *positive* I'd be on the Königstein on the 30th."

"As the big day approached, this nervousness became infectious," said Josie. "I had to stay in Berlin, but had arranged a secure phone link with Ahmed and we knocked various theories around. Got nowhere. Until the evening of the 29th, when… You tell him, Ahmed."

"You know how pilots check their aircraft before every flight," he began. "We don't usually do that with boats, but there's always a first time, so I went down to the quay in Dresden. It was late, no one else around. The steamer lay there gleaming, quiet, ready for next day's launch. I crept aboard. Gave it a good going over. Sure enough, well hidden, next to the fuel tank…"

"A bomb," said Josie.

I was bemused: "You found the bomb then and just left it?"

"I was about to tell the police," replied Ahmed, "but decided to phone Josie first."

"When Ahmed called, my natural reaction was also to tell the police," she said. "Then I thought again. No one blows up innocent people for the hell of it. There's always a *reason*, however bizarre it may seem to the rest of us. If Werner was responsible – and I could think of no one else – he *had* to expect a pay-off. Say what you like about the man, he was no fool. He…"

"Ahmed was to be the fall guy!" I exclaimed. Everything was falling into place. "The reason Werner was so desperate to have Ahmed on board was because without him the whole exercise was meaningless. Ahmed Aziz was to be the Islamic suicide bomber who would kill hundreds of innocent Germans. Manna from heaven for the German Democratic Right who would trumpet their message loud and clear: Vote for the DDR and we'll ban the buggers!"

"You've got it!" said Josie.

But I hadn't got it. Not all of it. I said: "I *still* don't understand why you didn't go straight to the police. Tell them your theory. It had to be Breitling. Have him arrested."

"What happens to criminals these days?" she asked. "We spend millions of taxpayers' money on a trial, after which the culprit spends a few years, again at taxpayers' expense, in a nice hotel with bars. Werner had ordered the death of my Jonny. I wanted *retribution*."

"You appear to have got it," I said. "How did you manage?"

"I asked Ahmed if he knew anything about bombs," replied Josie.

"As one does," I said.

Ahmed shrugged. "If you've lived in Iraq… Syria…"

"A man with technical expertise tends to know about these things," I suggested.

Ahmed nodded. "So I had a closer look at the bomb. Saw it was a simple device. Powerful, but easy to handle."

"How would Breitling have got his hands on it?" I asked.

"Through Feldmann," replied Josie. "The world's awash with military stuff and Sepp had all the underworld links."

I said: "As we saw from yesterday's fireworks display, you *didn't* make the bomb safe. Why not?"

"I did make it safe," replied Ahmed. "First the trigger, which was not a timer but activated by a signal. Then I removed the detonator. And told Josie."

"Who had a good long think," said Josie. "Although Breitling was obviously the mastermind, as usual he didn't want to soil his own hands and was farming out the job itself to Feldmann. Then, without warning, Feldmann became coy; kept replying to Werner's ever more feverish emails that his last job – killing me – had been so difficult he still had to lie low. Didn't dare return to Dresden. These were, of course, the emails I'd sent in Sepp's name. I don't know how long Werner kept believing them, but one thing would have been clear: if he wanted the job done, he'd have to do it himself."

Ahmed took over the story: "Josie and I had a long discussion. Breitling must have discarded the idea of a timer because of doubts about the Königstein's schedule. The boat might sail late; if they discovered another problem, even be indefinitely delayed. The only way to make sure the bomb went off in midstream was to have someone on shore, able to trigger the device at the right moment."

"This opened up the possibility of getting my own back," said Josie. "Seeing justice was really done. I could imagine Breitling watch the boat leave the quay; wait for the critical moment; at last everything is just right. He presses the button. Nothing! Tries again. And again; and again. The Königstein sails on, champagne glasses tinkling, band playing. What would Werner do?"

"He would follow the boat in his car, mad keen to discover what had gone wrong," I said.

"Exactly!" Josie was grinning broadly. "He would be past caring, his *only* ambition to find out why his lovely bomb had not gone off."

"He might even break through a police cordon and clamber aboard the boat in front of the assembled multitude," I said.

"He might indeed!" Josie was as happy as I'd ever seen her.

"How did you arrange a suitable reception?" I asked.

"With difficulty," replied Ahmed. "Mainly because of the time element. The Königstein was due to sail at two, so that only gave me the morning. Dresden is a big place with every type of shop, but even so I didn't think I was going to make it. In the end, with my new kit ready to install, I arrived with five minutes to spare."

"Must have taken a while to reassemble all the bits," I said. "And it was a short voyage. Weren't you pressed for time?"

"Not really. I'd done the fiddly part with the trigger on shore, and the detonator just slotted back into place. In fact, I had to hold back. Always treat explosives with care, so I delayed making it active until the last moment. It suited me that disembarkation took so long."

"Thanks to old ladies with fat sausage dogs," I said. "She and her pet dithered so long on the brink Fischer almost had a fit. I never realised she was doing you a favour."

"Job done, I was about last one off the boat," said Ahmed.

"And when everyone was well clear you pressed the button?"

Ahmed shook his head.

"*I* pressed the button," said Josie. "I'd come down from Berlin in the morning and didn't want Ahmed – or anyone else – to have the pleasure. Breitling and Feldmann had been the team that killed my Jonny. It should be me that made sure neither of them got away with it."

I asked: "What if Breitling had not done as you hoped? Had simply stayed ashore?"

"I don't trigger the bomb and the police find Werner's fingerprints all over it," she replied.

Ahmed added: I took the precaution of wearing gloves."

"Werner does not die, but goes to prison," concluded Josie.

"I can see why you don't want this story getting around," I said. "Two murders to your credit. It's good of you to trust me."

"Oh, I don't," she said. "I don't trust *anyone*. If you start blabbing, I'll be forced to tell them *my* truth: how you travelled to Berlin and stayed at the Hilton, while the two of us plotted Breitling's demise. Even in Germany, accessory to murder merits quite a long sentence."

Forty-Five

I should have been on cloud nine: a tragedy on the Elbe had been averted; Josie had avenged her husband's death; and Chief Inspector Fischer's big headache, the extremist DDR, had been decapitated.

Instead, I felt a profound sense of anti-climax. For weeks our lives had revolved around Breitling's machinations and the meaning of that mysterious date, the 30th September. Now it was back to normal. But I no longer did 'normal'.

Trudi had her hotel. And, unless I'd misjudged the mood, Josie had a new man. But I had... nothing. I'd set off four months earlier, in the wake of a mid-life, post-divorce crisis, in search of change and adventure. Been rewarded beyond expectation. But it was now October, gateway to winter, and I had no idea what to do next. I'd grown very fond of Trudi, but spending the rest of my natural as her bag carrier did not appeal.

So when she locked that dining room door for our ritual Jägermeister-fuelled debriefing, I was not my usual self.

Initially, I was able to hide my depression under the cloak of telling her what I'd learnt from my morning meeting with Josie and Ahmed. In accordance with Josie's wishes and common sense, this bore no relation to the truth.

I fed Trudi the accepted line: that Ahmed Aziz, as the engineer responsible for checking the steamer, only discovered the bomb when the cruise was under way. He called the police, then attempted to defuse the device, without success, finally being the last before the captain to leave. He left the bomb in such a delicate state that it came as no surprise when Breitling, disobeying police orders to stay clear, boarded the Königstein and set it off.

This account would not stand detailed scrutiny. Why had the Königstein not been beached as soon as the bomb was discovered? Maybe it had. The timeline was obscure. Records could also show that the call to the police had been made by a woman – in fact, Josie – not a man called Aziz. But the public loves heroics, so no one cared to question a few discrepancies.

When I'd finished this piece of fiction, Trudi brought up the thorny question of what I would be doing next. It had always been my stated intention to remain only until the 30th September conundrum had been resolved, then head for home.

"Home? What *had been* home I'd signed away to Maggie, with no intention of ever entering *that* lions' den again. It would be good to see the kids – 'kids'?, they were now almost middle-aged adults, for God's sake! But that would occupy me for at most a couple of days each. Which only left that old chestnut, a bit of consultancy work.

Incapable of deciding anything, I muttered about staying maybe a couple of weeks more 'to recover', then back to England.

"What about you?" I asked. "Apart from running the hotel, do *you* have any plans?"

"As usual, we'll stay open until the New Year," she replied. "Business is good during the festive season, then drops off to almost nothing. So we close in early January and take a couple of months off."

"What do you do then? Stay here?"

"Good heavens no! It's my one chance of some sun. The last few years I've been going to Maspalomas in Gran Canaria. Warm, nice weather, someone else to do all the hard work."

Seeing a chance to prolong my relationship with Trudi, I said: "How about a change for next year? Come with me. A cruise, perhaps?

She hesitated, tempted. The problem was obvious. So I said: "As my guest, I'll pay."

"Oh, I couldn't…"

I knew she would, so pressed on: "We could go somewhere really warm. The tropics in winter. The Caribbean"

No denials now, just a dreamy look in her eye. My imagination running riot, I continued:

"Why not a *world* cruise? Pacific, Australia, Magic of the Orient?"

"No, no, that would be far too long. But something shorter; maybe a month. I'll think about it."

I went to bed a happier man.

Forty-Six

Trudi thought about my suggestion for eight sleep-filled hours and next morning agreed that a month in the sun sounded lovely. Would welcome specific suggestions.

I could put up with three months of uncertainty in return for a promise of Trudi to myself in the New Year. As for my long-term future, that went back to the in-tray.

I'd left England in a rush months before and there were things back home that now needed my attention. I told Trudi I would leave in mid-October and return in time for the festive season, together with suggestions for escaping the European winter in January. Two days before I was due to leave, I received a call from Chief Inspector Fischer.

"What can I do for the hero of the hour?" I asked. The media had been generous in its praise for the man who had thwarted a 'massacre on the Elbe'.

He replied: "I'm often *blamed* for something I did not do,

so it's nice to be *praised* for something I also did *not* do."

"You're too modest," I said. "We couldn't have done it without you."

"*You* couldn't have done *what* without me?" He was quick to spot my slip of the tongue."

Cursing myself for virtually admitting we had been operating beyond the law, I stammered some nonsense: "Well... you know... Ahmed... Josie..."

"Don't worry, you're safe enough," said Fischer. "The Breitling case is closed. As is the death of Jonny Kästner, who was probably murdered by Feldmann on orders from Breitling. As I've also heard nothing more from Hungary regarding the body of Josef Feldmann, it's all over. But I like to cross the 't's and dot the 'i's, so to satisfy my personal curiosity..."

I could guess what was coming: "...Dinner at the Restaurant am Fluss?"

"Exactly. Shall we say tomorrow at seven?"

It was too cold now for the outside terrace, so we found ourselves again seated beneath the German Monarch of the Glen, supping on trout and wine that was well up to the house's high standard. Fischer was his usual natty self, more like a silver screen idol than a plodding cop.

"You only want to see me to practise your English," I joked.

"That as well. But the Kästner-Breitling case had some strange features which you might like to comment on."

"Or not."

He nodded. "Of course. You're perfectly entitled to 'Take the Fifth', as our American friends would say."

"What strange features are you talking about?"

"Well, the Feldmann case may have ended on someone else's patch, but we're obviously still interested. That dog... what was his name again?"

"Attila."

"Yes, Attila. People don't usually kill their own pets and certainly not in such a savage way, so we can assume Feldmann was responsible. Frau Molnar might well have wanted revenge, but she was not capable of the frenzied type of attack that finished off Feldmann, so a third person must have been involved."

"I believe you suggested a German underworld connection," I said. "Which the Hungarian police were following up."

"A theory purely for public consumption. We both know who that third person is, but the crime was committed in Hungary, where they seem to have lost interest; and I've no intention of stirring things. However, there's also the puzzle of the knives. Feldmann died from multiple stab wounds, as did the dog, yet not a single knife was found at the scene. Do you have any ideas?"

I could see no harm in throwing Fischer a bone, as it were, so replied: "There could have been *two* knives. One killed Feldmann, was cleaned and returned to its original place. A second knife was used against Attila, then thrown into the Danube."

Fischer agreed that this seemed a good explanation and got down to dismembering his trout.

After a while of silent eating, I enquired: "Was there anything else?"

"I never realised the Königstein emails referred to the boat, not the place," he replied. "How did Josie Kästner find out?"

"Even though hiding in Berlin, she read the Dresden press, where she saw the item about the voyage of the new steamer; then put two and two together. For you, based in Berlin, the news item was easy to miss."

"There's also the mystery of the phone call," said Fischer. "The accepted version is that it was Mr. Aziz who made it, yet the voice I heard was a lady, recognisably Mrs. Kästner. When she called I had all my assets in the *wrong* Königstein. She gave me just enough time to leap into the police chopper and get myself to the *right* Königstein. Then, as soon as everyone was off the boat, it exploded. It was all too pat. As though I'd been caught up in a military operation."

"You're too suspicious," I said.

"That's my job. I'd also like to know how *you* appeared on the scene *before* me. How long in advance had you known?"

The questions were becoming uncomfortable, so I replied: "I'd better take the fifth – say nothing."

"I thought you might. Let me try you with another: Aziz claims he only discovered the bomb *after* they had sailed; that he wrestled to defuse it, had almost succeeded, but then had to leave the device in a dangerous state when ordered off the boat. Doesn't this also strike you as too pat? In fact, unlikely?"

I decided to be honest. Replied: "Yes, it does."

Fischer looked at me, surprised. Realising I was not going to add to this, he said: "The Königstein case is effectively closed. Everyone is… I believe the word is 'chuffed'. A satisfactory outcome, with no need for any prosecutions. Police work is not really about putting people behind bars, but maintaining law and order. Emphasis on the word 'order'. Nothing worse than anarchy. But I like to *understand*. Can you tell me anything more that might help me?"

"Off the record?"

"Absolutely off the record."

I gathered my thoughts: "The Good Book is confusing. On one page it's okay to demand an eye for an eye; on the next we should turn the other cheek. We may have become slightly more civilised over the centuries, watching the telly rather than public executions, but there's a feeling now that we're turning too many cheeks. Retribution remains a basic human emotion."

"Even when it means taking the law into one's own hands?"

"If the law is unable to deliver, yes. In the case we're talking about, most people would agree justice has been done. And order has been maintained. What more could you want?"

The Chief Inspector nodded slowly. "What more, indeed."

He was lost in thought for a while. I let him think on.

At last he said: "I've enjoyed our meetings; this one being the last, I'm afraid. Our business is concluded and I'm being moved to another post."

"Promotion?

A smile and modest inclination of the head.

"Well deserved," I said. "I'll also miss our little chats."

Even though I had now spent several hours in total talking to Helmut Fischer, I realised I still knew nothing about the man behind the Chief Inspector label. Was he married? Did he have a family? I was wondering whether to venture into his private domain when he beat me to it.

"As a parting gift, would you allow me to offer some insights you might find useful?" he asked.

"Of course." I couldn't imagine what he meant.

"As I've said before, information is everything, so our Bundeskriminalamt files are thick with data about the leading players in our recent drama. Two, in particular, you might like to know more about: Josie Kästner and Trudi Lindtner."

"I can understand why you're interested in Josie, but what has Trudi done?"

"Nothing in recent years; a model citizen by all accounts. But our files go back a long way, and during the DDR era – that's the East German state, not the political party – a certain Trudi Zinn was attracting a lot of attention."

"Yes, she told me she married one of the Stasi bosses. Old enough to be her father, as she put it."

Fischer smiled. "No doubt she gave the impression she was a naïve young thing who happened to catch the eye of a political bigwig."

"She said Lindtner was one of the local leaders."

"Franz Lindtner was a mid-level apparatchik with little clout and no ability," said Fischer. "Trudi Zinn was a Party Youth leader, a stunner to look at, who was determined to go places. *She* was the hunter; Lindtner her prey. A first step up the ladder of influence."

"What happened?"

"The wall came down. That's what happened. Trudi Lindtner, as she now was, found she had hitched her wagon to a caravan that was going nowhere."

But she'd married into one of the old families," I said. "She did at least have the hotel."

Fischer nodded. "And she's done well. Considering."

"Considering what?"

"That East Germany, like the whole of the Communist world, was bankrupt. Skint. In the gospel according to Saint Marx, money was evil. Although many of the state's assets were returned to the private sector when the wall came down, there was hardly any cash to develop these assets. West Germany had to pour billions into the East to get it going. It was never enough."

"You're saying Trudi could have done with more investment for the hotel?"

"I'm saying young Trudi Zinn was that rare commodity in the Communist world – someone with ambition. I'd guess Trudi Lindtner still has something of that left in her."

"As her middle-aged bellboy I can vouch for the fact that the hotel could do with some lifts," I said. "Apart from that…"

"I'm thinking more of wider investment opportunities," said Fischer. "I happen to know there's an old barracks for sale, on the edge of town with a riverside view. It's a large plot, which I also happen to know Frau Lindtner would love to develop. Planning permission has been granted to tear down the unsightly barracks and replace them with a brand new hotel and conference centre. Open throughout the year; a huge asset to the community."

"She never said…"

"That's because she's a proud woman. The complete project will cost upwards of seven million Euros. A fantastic opportunity, but she can't raise the cash."

I couldn't help laughing: "Sometimes, Helmut, you're ridiculously transparent."

"Glad to hear it."

"I didn't know your job description included being a marriage broker."

"I prefer finance broker. On the one hand, we have a local entrepreneur with all the right connections, thwarted by lack of cash; on the other, there's a foreign Prince Charming with exactly the assets our Cinderella lacks: money and business experience. Seems to me the two should get together."

"You make a persuasive case, which I shall certainly consider. You also mentioned Josie Kästner; you're surely not suggesting I hop into bed with *another* lady…"

"I fancy Mrs. Kästner already has a new partner; but they might welcome some help. I'm told the sole surviving founder of the German Democratic Right Party is leaving politics…"

"I'm not surprised after what she's been through. At the moment the two of them are in Spain – Costa del Sol, recovering from their ordeal; so we're again looking after Karl, who's coming to regard the hotel as his second home."

"That's good news," said Fischer. "Because when Josie and Ahmed return they'll need some work."

"Ahmed empties dustbins," I pointed out.

"None too satisfying for an engineer. Especially one who can defuse bombs."

"Nearly defuse. It exploded, remember."

"*After* having once been made harmless. I'm not a complete idiot, Ed."

I shrugged. "So Ahmed could do with a better job. What do you suggest?

"Josie also needs a new lease of life. She's been running the DDR virtually single handed, so is obviously a good organiser. And she fooled me, which doesn't often happen. So I suggest the two of them be considered for the job of running the Hotel Lindtner when Trudi has her hands full overseeing the big new project."

You *are* taking a lot for granted."

"It's called planning. Do you see any serious obstacles?"

I spread my hands, helplessly. "Thousands of obstacles. But it'll work! I'll make damned sure it does."

Fischer gave a satisfied smile. "I knew I could count on you. Or rather, on Trudi. When she weaves her spell, you're doomed."

I loved being doomed. It would solve my two big problems: how to occupy my time and whether to stay with Trudi.

"Helmut, you're a genius!" I couldn't contain myself.

"All in a day's work for the average plod," he said. But I could see he was pleased.

We spent the rest of the meal plotting how to achieve my aims: getting Trudi to accept me as the financial half of a business partnership and – should they accept – training Josie and Ahmed in how to run the hotel.

As we parted, I wished the Chief Inspector luck in his new post; and regretted he would be leaving the area for his native Frankfurt – the one on the Main.

"The pleasure is all mine…" He shook my hand. "… Engländer."

It was the last word he spoke to me. And the first time he'd used a word in German. As Chief Inspector Fischer drove off, it struck me I still didn't know whether he was married; or had a family; or anything.

Forty-Seven

It's only twelve months from the day I first set foot in 'Die Stadt', but it feels as though I've been here forever. It's home.

My suggestion of four months' winter warmth on a cruise ship, a full circumnavigation, had been tempting, but rejected. Like all true entrepreneurs, Trudi was keen to get on with it. We'd managed a month in the Caribbean, then come back to make our dream a reality.

With my collateral in the bank, the finances had quickly fallen into place, the old plans dusted off and improved. The barracks would go, the whole area close to the river returned to grass; this was, after all, a flood plain. Two hundred metres inland, with spectacular views over the Elbe, would be the Lindtnerhof, a state-of-the-art hotel and conference centre, complete with two swimming pools (inside and out), spa, cinema, etcetera.

Josie and Ahmed, now Mr. and Mrs. Aziz, needed little persuasion to join our team. Josie could run anything, while her new husband turned out to be a capable and charming front-of-house for the old Lindtner hotel. His appointment was trumpeted as how migrants *could* be successfully integrated into the wider community, but in truth Ahmed Aziz, well-educated and speaking fluent German, was hardly typical; the real problem remained those with little to offer.

As for Karl, the lad who had inadvertently welcomed me to my new home, it was a pleasure watching him grow up. We had been to Berlin a couple of times to see his team, Hertha, in action. In return, I'd managed to scrounge two tickets for the Emirates, where we'd watched a post-Wenger Arsenal on rampant form.

The Lindtnerhof is due for completion early next year. Our marketing team is even now preparing the brochures. May we send you a copy when they are ready?